Millie watched him—*this man she loved*—wondering what was going through his mind. As if reading her thoughts, he turned. The ever-present chemistry flickered across the room, resurrecting a connection that had never died.

"I don't want a divorce. I want a wife. I want *you*. Come back to me," he said hoarsely, his eyes glittering darkly in his handsome face. "Come back to me, and this time we'll get it right."

Millie felt her stomach drop.

"You can't be serious—" Her barely audible whisper increased the tension in his powerful frame.

"It's still there," he growled. "What we shared. You can feel it. I can feel it. It hasn't gone away. I doubt it's ever going to go away."

"Leandro—"

SARAH MORGAN was born in Wiltshire and started writing at the age of eight, when she produced an autobiography of her hamster.

At the age of eighteen she traveled to London to train as a nurse in one of London's top teaching hospitals, and she describes what happened in those years as extremely happy and definitely censored!

She worked in a number of areas after she qualified, but her favorite was A&E, where she found the work stimulating and fun. Nowhere else in the hospital environment did she encounter such good teamwork between doctors and nurses.

By now her interests had moved from hamsters to men, and she started writing romance fiction. Her first completed manuscript, written after the birth of her first child, was rejected by Harlequin® Books, but the comments were encouraging, so she tried again, and on the third attempt her manuscript *Worth the Risk* was accepted unchanged. She describes receiving the acceptance letter as one of the best moments of her life, after meeting her husband and having her two children.

Sarah still works part-time in a health-related industry and spends the rest of the time with her family, trying to squeeze in writing whenever she can. She is an enthusiastic skier and walker and loves outdoor life.

POWERFUL GREEK, UNWORLDLY WIFE

SARAH MORGAN

~ INNOCENT WIVES ~

HARLEQUIN®

TORONTO • NEW YORK • LONDON
AMSTERDAM • PARIS • SYDNEY • HAMBURG
STOCKHOLM • ATHENS • TOKYO • MILAN • MADRID
PRAGUE • WARSAW • BUDAPEST • AUCKLAND

Recycling programs
for this product may
not exist in your area.

ISBN-13: 978-0-373-52745-8

POWERFUL GREEK, UNWORLDLY WIFE

First North American Publication 2009.

Copyright © 2009 by Sarah Morgan.

www.eHarlequin.com

Printed in U.S.A.

POWERFUL GREEK, UNWORLDLY WIFE

CHAPTER ONE

LEANDRO DEMETRIOS, billionaire banker and the subject of a million hopeful female fantasies, dragged the 'A' list Hollywood actress through the doorway of his exclusive London townhouse and slammed the door shut on the rain and the bank of waiting photographers.

The woman was laughing, her eyes wide with feminine appreciation. 'Did you see their faces? You scared them half to death! I feel safer with you than I do with my bodyguards. *And* you have bigger muscles.' She slid her hand up his arm, her manicured fingernails lingering on the solid curve of his biceps. 'Why didn't we just use the back entrance?'

'Because I refuse to creep around my own house. And because you like to be seen.'

'Well, we've certainly been seen.' The fact evidently pleased her. 'You'll be all over the papers tomorrow for terrorising the paparazzi.'

Leandro frowned. 'I only read the financial pages.'

'And that's the bit I *don't* read,' she sighed. 'The only thing I know about money is how to spend it. You, on the other hand, know how to make it by the bucketload, and that makes you my type of guy. Now, *stop* looking all moody and dangerous and smile! I'm only in town for twenty-four hours and we need to make the most of the time.' Her lashes lowered provocatively. 'So, Leandro Demetrios, my very own sexy Greek billionaire. *Finally* we're alone. What are we going to do with our evening?'

Leandro removed his jacket and threw it carelessly over the back of a chair. 'If that's a serious question, you can leave right now.' His remark drew a gurgle of delighted laughter from the woman clinging to his arm.

'No one else dares to speak to me the way you do. It's one of the things I love most about you. You're not starstruck and that's so refreshing for someone like me.' The tip of her tongue traced the curve of her glossy lips. 'If I told you I was going to kiss you goodnight and go back to my hotel, what would you do?'

'Dump you.' Leandro's bow-tie landed on top of the jacket. 'But we both know that isn't going to happen. You want what I want, so stop playing games and get up those stairs. My bedroom is on the first floor. Last door on the left.'

'*So-o* macho.' Laughing, she smouldered in his direction. 'According to a poll just last week, you're now officially the world's sexiest man.'

Bored by the conversation, Leandro's only response was to close his fingers around her tiny wrist and pull her towards the staircase.

She gave a gasp of shocked delight. 'You honestly don't care what anyone thinks about you, do you? Indifference is *such* a turn-on. And when it comes to indifference, you wrote the manual.' She walked with a slow, swaying motion that she'd perfected for the cameras. 'There's a special chemistry between us. I can feel it.'

'It's called lust,' Leandro drawled, and she shot him a challenging look.

'Haven't you ever had a serious relationship with a woman? I heard you were married for a short time.'

Leandro stilled. *A very short time.* 'These days I prefer variety.'

'Honey, I can give you variety.' She used the soft, smoky voice that earned her millions of dollars per movie. 'And I'm just dying to know whether everything they say about you is true. I know you're super-bright and that you drive your fancy cars *way* too fast, but what I want to know is just how much of a bad boy you really are when it comes to women.'

'As bad as they come,' Leandro said smoothly, his hand locked around her slender wrist as he led her up the stairs. 'Which makes this your lucky night.'

'Then lead on, handsome.' She kept pace with him, a smile on her full, glossy mouth. 'You have a lot of art on your walls. Great investment. Are they original? I hate anything fake.'

'Of course you do.' Leandro focused on her surgically enhanced breasts with wry amusement. At a rough estimate he guessed that ninety per cent of her was fake. The short time he'd spent with her had been enough to prove to him that she was so used to playing other people, she'd forgotten how to be herself.

And that was fine by him.

As far as he was concerned, the shallower the better. At least you knew what you were dealing with and you adjusted your expectations accordingly.

'Oh, my! Only you would have a picture of a naked woman at the head of your staircase.' Stopping dead, she gazed up at the huge canvas and wrinkled her nose with disapproval. 'Strange choice for a man who surrounds himself with beauty. Isn't she rather fat for your tastes?'

Leandro's gaze lingered on the celebrated Renaissance masterpiece that had only recently returned from being on loan to a major gallery. 'When she was alive, it was fashionable to be curvy.'

The girl stared blankly at the exquisite brush strokes. 'I guess they didn't know about low carbs.'

'Curves were a sign of wealth,' Leandro murmured. 'It meant you had enough to eat.'

Throwing him a look of blank incomprehension, the actress stepped closer to the painting and Leandro's fingers tightened like a vice around her wrist.

'Touch it and we'll have half the Metropolitan police force keeping us company tonight.'

'It's that valuable?' Her knowing gaze turned to his and she licked her lips. 'You are one rich, powerful guy. Now, why is that such a turn-on, I wonder? It isn't as if I care about your money.'

'Of course you don't,' Leandro said, his tone dry because he knew full well that her lovers were expected to pay handsomely for the privilege of escorting her. 'We both know you're interested in me because I'm kind to old ladies and animals.'

'You like animals?'

Looking down into those famous blue eyes, Leandro's own eyes gleamed. 'I've always had a soft spot for dumb creatures.'

'That's so attractive. I love a tough man with a gentle side.' She slid her arms round his neck like bindweed around a plant. 'Do you realise we've had dinner three times and you haven't told me a single thing about yourself?'

'Do you realise that we've had dinner three times and you haven't eaten a single thing?' Skilfully steering the conversation away from the personal, Leandro smoothly released the zip on her dress and she sucked in a breath.

'You don't mess around, do you?'

'Let's just say I've had enough of verbal foreplay,' Leandro purred, sliding the dress over her shoulders in a practised movement. He frowned slightly as his fingers brushed hard bones rather than soft flesh.

'People pay good money to see this body of mine up on the screen.' She scraped her nails gently down his arm. 'And you, Leandro Demetrios, are getting it for free.'

Hardly, he thought, looking at the earrings she was wearing. *Earrings he'd given her at the beginning of the evening.* 'Shame you're not sold by the kilogram,' he said idly, 'because then you wouldn't cost me anything.'

'Thank you.' Assuming his remark was a compliment, she smiled. 'You, on the other hand, would cost a woman a fortune because muscle is heavier than fat and you have to be the most impressively built man I've ever met. And you're so damned confident. Is that because you're Greek?'

'No. It's because I'm me. I take what I want.' He took her chin in his fingers, his eyes steely. 'And when I've finished with it, I drop it.'

She shuddered deliciously. 'With no apology to anyone. Cold, ruthless, single-minded…'

'Are we talking about me or you?' Leandro removed the diamond clip securing her hair. 'I'm confused.'

'I'm willing to bet you've never been confused about a single thing in your life, you wicked boy.' Smiling, she dragged her finger over his lower lip. 'Tell me something personal about yourself. Just one thing. This latest story about you being the father of that baby—is it true? The papers are full of it.'

Not by the flicker of an eyelid did Leandro reveal his sudden tension. 'Are those the same papers that accused you of being a lesbian?'

'The difference is that my people issued a stern denial—you've said nothing.'

'I've never felt the need to explain my life to anyone.'

'So does that mean it isn't your child?' She lowered her lashes. 'Or are you such a stud you don't even *know?* You're not giving anything away, are you? Tell me something about *you.*'

'You want to know something about me?' Leandro eased her dress down her painfully thin body and lowered his mouth to the base of her throat. 'If you give me your heart, I'll break it. Remember that, *agape mou.* And I won't do it gently.' The warmth of his tongue brought a soft gasp to her lips and she tipped her head back with a shiver.

'If you're trying to scare me, you're not succeeding.' Her eyes were dark with arousal. 'I love a man who knows how to be a man. Especially when that man has a sensitive side.'

'I don't have a sensitive side.' Leandro's voice was hard as he lowered his forehead to hers. For a moment he stared into her wild, excited eyes, his breath mingling with hers. 'I don't care about anyone or anything. Lie down in my bed and I'll guarantee you fantastic sex, but nothing else. So if you're looking for happy ever after, you've taken a wrong turning.'

'Happy ever after is for movies. It's my day job. At night, I prefer to live for the moment.' Squirming against him, she lifted her hand and stroked his rough jaw. 'I should make you shave before you touch me, but I like the way it makes you look. You are so damn handsome, Leandro, it shouldn't be allowed,' she breathed, lifting her mouth to his. 'My last leading man needed satellite navigation to find his way round a woman's body. I have a feeling you won't suffer from the same problem.'

'I've always had a very good sense of direction.' Leandro backed her against the door and the actress gasped her approval.

'Oh, yes…' Panting, she wrenched at his shirt, sending buttons flying. With a low moan of desire she pushed the shirt off his shoulders and let it fall to the floor. 'Your body is incredible. I'm *definitely* going to get you a part in my next movie. I want you *now.*'

Having reached the part of the evening that interested him, Leandro scooped her up, strode purposefully towards the bed and then froze because his bed was already occupied.

The woman sat glaring at him, her eyes a fierce blue in a face as pale as his dress shirt. She'd obviously been caught in the rain because her thin cardigan clung to her body and her long hair curled damply past her shoulders like tongues of red fire.

Given the state she was in, she should have looked pathetic, but she didn't. She looked angry—the blaze of her eyes and the angle of her chin warning him that this wasn't going to be a gentle reunion.

It was as if a small, unexploded firework had landed in his bedroom and Leandro felt a dart of surprise because he'd never seen her angry before—*hadn't known she was capable of anger.*

He'd been on the receiving end of her injured dignity, her silent reproach and her agonised pain. He'd witnessed her disappointment and contempt. But a good healthy dose of old-fashioned anger had been missing from their relationship.

She hadn't thought that what they had was worth fighting for.

His own anger bubbled up from nowhere, threatening his usual control, and the emotion caught him by surprise because he'd thought he had himself well in hand.

Unfinished business, he thought grimly, and was about to speak when the actress gave a shocked squeak and tightened her grip on his neck.

'Who's *she?* You bastard! When you said you were going

to hurt me, I didn't expect it to be that quick,' she snarled. 'How *dare* you see someone else while you're with me? I expect my relationships to be exclusive.'

Surprised to realise that he'd forgotten he had the actress in his arms, Leandro lowered her unceremoniously to the floor. 'I don't do relationships.' *Not any more.*

'What about her?' Balancing on her vertiginous heels, the actress shot him a poisonous look. 'Does *she* know that?'

'Oh, yes.' Leandro was watching the girl on the bed and his humourless smile was entirely at his own expense. 'She wouldn't trust me as far as she could throw me, isn't that right, Millie?'

Her eyes were two hot pools of blame and he ground his teeth. *Fight me,* he urged silently. *If that's really what you think of me, stand up and scratch my eyes out. Don't just sit there. And don't walk out like you did the first time.*

But she didn't move. She sat in frozen silence, her eyes telling him that nothing had changed.

The actress made an outraged noise. 'So you *do* know her! Surprising. She doesn't look your type,' she said spitefully. 'She needs to fire her stylist. That natural look is *so* yesterday. This season is all about grooming.' She snatched her dress from the floor and held it against her. 'How did she get in here, anyway? Your security is really tight. I suppose no one noticed her.'

Nothing killed sexual arousal faster than female bitchiness, Leandro thought idly, regretting the impulse that had driven him to invite the actress home. The woman's tongue was as sharp as the bones poking out through her almost transparent flesh.

'Well? Are you going to throw her out?' The actress's voice turned from sultry to shrill and Leandro studied the girl sitting on his bed, noting the flush on her cheeks and the accusation in her eyes.

He met that gaze full on, with accusation of his own.

Silent communication raged between them and the atmosphere was so thick with tension that both of them forgot about the third person in the room until she stamped her foot.

'*Leandro?*'

'No,' he said harshly. 'I'm not going to throw her out.' The timing wasn't what he would have chosen but now she was here, he had no intention of letting her go. *Not until they'd had the conversation she'd walked away from a year earlier.*

The actress gave a gasp of disbelief. 'You're choosing that plain, bedraggled, badly dressed nobody over me?'

Leandro sent his date a cold, assessing glance that would have triggered shivers of trepidation through any one of the people who worked for him or knew him well. 'Yes. At least that way I'm guaranteed a soft landing when we tumble onto that mattress. No bones. No claws.'

The actress gasped. 'I won't be treated like this!' Delivering a performance worthy of an Oscar, she wriggled back into her dress and tossed her head in anger. 'You told me you weren't involved with anyone and I believed you! I'm obviously more of a fool than I look.'

Deciding that it was wisest not to respond to that particular statement, Leandro stayed silent, his gaze returned to the girl sitting on his bed. In that single, hotly charged moment he felt the blaze of raw sexual chemistry erupt between them. It was elemental, basic and primitive—the connection so powerful that it was beyond control or understanding. Recognising that fact, she gave a murmur of denial, her expression one of sick contempt as she dragged her gaze from his.

Vibrating with desperation, the actress sent a look of

longing towards Leandro's bare, bronzed torso. 'I know you didn't expect to see her here. I know women throw themselves at you. Just get rid of her and we can start again. I forgive you.'

Propelled by a need to ensure that forgiveness would never be forthcoming, Leandro urged her towards the door. 'You need to learn to play nicely with the other girls. I don't mind knives in my boardroom but I do find them shockingly un-comfortable in my bedroom.'

Her face scarlet, the actress snatched her phone out of her tiny jewelled handbag. 'All the rumours about you are true, Leandro Demetrios. You *are* cold and heartless and just missed your chance to have the one thing every man in the world wants.'

'And that would be?' Leandro raised an eyebrow, deliber-ately provocative. 'Peace and quiet?'

The actress simmered like milk coming to the boil. 'Me! And next time you're in LA, don't bother calling. And you.' She glared at the girl on the bed. 'If you think he'll ever be faithful to you, you're crazy.' Checking that the diamond earrings were still in place, she stormed from the room and several moments later Leandro heard a distant thud as the front door slammed closed.

Silence closed in on them.

'If you're going to cry, you can leave now,' Leandro drawled softly. 'If you choose to wait in my bedroom, you deserve to get hurt.'

'I'm not going to cry over you. And I'm not hurt,' she said stiffly. 'I'm past being hurt.'

Then she'd done better than him, Leandro reflected grimly. 'Why are you here?'

'You know why I'm here. I—I've come to take the baby.'

Of course, the baby. He'd been a fool to think anything else, and yet for a moment…

Leandro curled one hand into a fist, surprised to discover that his thick protective layer of cynicism could still be breached.

'I was asking what you're doing in my bedroom at midnight.' Strolling across to the bedroom door, he pushed it shut. He trusted his staff, but he was also sharp enough to know that this story was the juiciest morsel the media had savoured for a long time. They were slavering outside his house, waiting for something to feast on.

And everyone had their price.

He'd learned that unpalatable truth in the harshest way possible, and at an age when most children were still playing with toys.

'I'm intrigued as to how you got past my security.'

'I'm still your wife, Leandro. Even if you've forgotten that fact.'

'I haven't forgotten.' Keeping his gaze neutral, he looked at her. 'You really pick your moments. Thanks to you, my night of hot sex just walked through that door.'

Her slender shoulders stiffened, her back rigid. 'I'm sure you'll find a replacement fast enough. You always do.' Her chest rose and fell as she breathed rapidly and then her eyes flew to his, bright with accusation and pain. 'You *are* a complete and utter bastard, she's right about that.'

'I've never heard you use bad language before. It doesn't suit you.' Leandro strolled across the bedroom and lifted a bottle of whisky from a small table. *Funny,* he thought, *that his hand was so steady.* 'And I don't understand why you're angry. You walked out on our marriage, not me. I was in it for the long haul.'

'Only you could make it sound like an endurance test. It's nice to know you had such a positive view of our relationship. No wonder it didn't last five minutes. You're even more unfeeling than I thought you were—' She broke off, as if she was trying to control herself. 'You're horribly, *horribly* insensitive.'

'I'm living my life. What's insensitive about that?' Leandro's hand remained steady as he poured. 'There was a vacancy in my bed and I filled it. In the circumstances, you can hardly blame me for that. Drink?'

'No, thank you.'

'Such perfect English manners.' Leandro gave a humourless laugh as he lifted the glass. 'Don't tell me—alcohol is fattening and you're watching your weight.'

'No. I'm watching my tongue. If I drink, I'll tell you exactly what I think of you and right now that might not be a good idea because what I think of you isn't very flattering.'

His hand stilled on the glass. 'Don't hold back on my account. It's interesting to know you're capable of expressing what you're feeling providing you're sufficiently provoked. Just for the record, I actually prefer confrontation to retreat.'

She closed her eyes, misery visible in every angle of her pretty face. 'I *hate* confrontation. I didn't come here to argue with you.'

'I'm sure you didn't.' Leandro examined the golden liquid in his glass. 'You don't talk about problems, do you, Millie? And you were certainly never interested in fixing the problems in our relationship. It's so much easier to just walk away when things become awkward.'

'How *dare* you say that to me when *you're* the one who—?' She broke off as if she couldn't even bear to say it, and his mouth tightened.

'I'm the one who what?' His silky soft voice was in direct contrast to the passion in hers. 'Spell it out, Millie. Come on—let's hear what I'm guilty of.'

'You *know* what! And I didn't come here to talk about that. 'You're a—a…' She appeared to struggle with her breath and he gave her a long look.

'You really must learn to finish your sentences, *agape mou.*' His tone bored, he offered no sympathy. As far as he was concerned, she deserved none. He'd given her a chance. He'd given her something he'd never offered a woman before. And she'd thrown it back in his face. 'I'm cold and heartless, isn't that right, Millie? Wasn't that what you were going to say?'

'I wish I'd never met you.'

'Now, that's just childish.' Leandro suppressed a yawn and she looked away.

'Our relationship was a disaster.'

'I wouldn't say that. For a short time you were a revelation in bed, and I was reasonably entertained by your gift for saying the wrong thing at the wrong time.'

'It's called telling the truth.' She glared at him through lashes spiked with rain. 'Where I come from, that's what people do. They tell it like it is and that way there's no confusion. When someone says, "Lovely to see you," they mean it. In *your* world when someone says, "Lovely to see you," they certainly *don't* mean it. They kiss you even though they hate you.'

Leandro added ice to his glass. 'It's a standard social greeting.'

'It's superficial—everything about your world is!' She sprang off the bed and walked towards him, her eyes flashing fire. 'And that included our relationship.'

'I'm not the one who called time on our marriage.'

'Yes, you did!' Angry and hurt, she faced him. 'You blame me for walking out, but what did you think I'd do, Leandro?

Did you think I'd say, "Don't worry, that's fine by me"?' Her voice rose, trembling and thickened by pain. 'Did you think I'd turn a blind eye? Maybe that's what women do in your world, but that isn't the sort of marriage I want. You slept with another woman and not just any woman.' Her breathing was jagged. 'My sister. *My own sister.*' Her distress was so obvious that Leandro gave a frown.

'You're working yourself up into a state.'

'Please don't pretend you care about my feelings because you've already amply demonstrated that you don't.' Holding herself together by a thread, she wrapped her arms around her body and met his gaze.

Brave, he thought absently, part of him intrigued by the sudden strength he saw in her. Yes, she was upset. But she wasn't caving in, was she? He hadn't known that she possessed a layer of steel. By the end of their relationship he'd come to the conclusion that she was so lightweight that the only thing preventing her from being blown away was the weight of his money in her handbag.

Leandro's hand tightened on his glass and then he lifted it to his lips and drained it. Then he placed the glass carefully on the table in front of him.

'Given the circumstances of your departure, I'm surprised you chose to come back.'

Sinking back onto the side of the bed, the fight seemed to go out of her and she suddenly looked incredibly tired. Tired, wet, beaten. 'If you thought I wouldn't then you know even less about me than I thought you did.'

'I never knew you.' It had been a fantasy. An illusion. *Or maybe a delusion?*

'And whose fault is that? You didn't *want* to know me, did you? You weren't interested in *me*—just in sex, and when that—' She broke off and took a breath, clearly searching for the words she wanted. 'I wasn't right for you. To start with you liked the fact that I was "different". I was just an ordinary girl, living in the country, working on her parents' farm. Unsophisticated. But the novelty wore off, didn't it, Leandro? You wanted me to fit into your life. Your world. And I didn't.'

Watching her so closely, he was able to detect the exact moment when anger turned to awareness.

Her eyes slid to his bare, bronzed shoulders and then back to his. It was like putting a match to kerosene. The chemistry that had been simmering exploded to dangerous levels and she turned away with a murmur of frustration, although whether it was with herself or him, he wasn't sure. 'Don't you dare, Leandro! Don't you *dare* look at me like that—as if everything hasn't changed between us.'

'You were looking at me.'

'Because you're standing there half-naked!'

'Does that bother you?'

'No, it doesn't.' She rubbed her hands up and down her arms, trying to warm them. 'I don't feel anything for you any more.'

'Oh, you feel plenty for me, Millie,' Leandro said grimly, 'and that's the problem, isn't it? You hate the fact that you can feel that way. A woman like you shouldn't find herself hopelessly attracted to a bad boy like me. It's not quite decent, is it?'

'I'm not here because of you.'

'Of course you're not.' His tone caustic, he watched as she flinched away from his words. 'You wouldn't have made the journey for something as trivial as the survival of our marriage, would you? That was never important to you.' Filled with contempt, Leandro lifted the glass, wondering how much whisky it was going to take to dull what he was feeling.

'Are you drunk?'

'Unfortunately, no, not yet.' He eyed the glass. 'But I'm working on it.'

'You're totally irresponsible.'

'I'm working on that, too.' He was about to lift the glass to his lips when he noticed that the sole of her boot was starting to come away. Remembering how obsessive she'd been about her appearance, he frowned. 'You look awful.'

'Most people would look awful compared with the cream of Hollywood,' she said tartly. She lifted her hand and he thought she was going to smooth her damp hair, but then she let her hand drop as if she'd decided it wasn't worth the effort. 'She's very beautiful.'

He heard the pain in her voice and gritted his teeth. 'Jealousy was the one aspect of our relationship at which you consistently excelled.'

'You're *so* unkind.'

Leandro discovered that his fingers had curled themselves into a fist. 'Unkind?' His mouth tightened. 'Yes, I'm unkind.'

'Do you love her?'

'Now you're getting personal.'

'Of course I'm getting personal! Did my sis—?' Her voice cracked and she cleared her throat. 'Did…Becca know you were seeing the actress?'

The mention of that name made Leandro want to drain the bottle of whisky, as did the unspoken accusation behind her words. 'Are you blaming me for the fact that your sister crashed the car while under the influence of drink and drugs?'

'She drank because you rejected her! She was suffering from depression.'

Thinking about what he knew, Leandro gave a humourless smile. 'I'll just bet she was.'

She sprang to her feet and crossed the room with the grace of a dancer. 'Don't you *dare* speak about the dead like that! If anyone was responsible for my sister's fragile mental state, it's you. You broke her heart.'

And Leandro committed the unpardonable sin. He laughed. And that grim humour cost him.

She slapped him.

Then she put her hand against her throat and stepped backwards, as if she couldn't believe what she'd done. Her skin was so pale she reminded him of something conjured from a child's fairy story.

'I should probably apologise but I'm not going to,' she whispered, her fingers pressed against her slender neck. 'Do you know the most hurtful part of all this? You don't even care. You destroyed our marriage for sex. It didn't even *mean* anything. If you'd loved her maybe, just maybe, I would have been able to understand all this, but for you it was just physical.'

'As a matter of interest, did you say any of this to her?'

'Yes. Actually, I did. I went to see her just after she was admitted to that clinic in Arizona. I...' She rubbed her fingers across her forehead. 'I needed to try and understand. She confessed that she was so madly in love with you that she wasn't thinking clearly.'

'She knew exactly what she was doing,' Leandro said flatly. 'The only person your sister ever loved was herself. That was probably the only thing we ever had in common.'

'That's a very cynical attitude.'

'I'm a cynical guy.'

'So you wrecked our marriage for a woman you don't even care about.'

'I didn't wreck our marriage, *agape mou*,' Leandro spoke

softly, his eyes fixing on her white face, as he hammered home his barb. 'You did that. All by yourself.'

If he'd hit her, she couldn't have looked more shocked. 'How can you say that? What did you expect? I'm not the sort of woman who can turn a blind eye while her husband has an affair. Especially when the woman involved was his wife's sister. You made her pregnant, Leandro! How was I supposed to overlook that?' Visibly distressed, she turned away. 'What I don't understand is why, if you wanted my sister, did you bother with me at all?'

Leandro let that question hover in the air. 'And does the fact that you don't understand help you draw any conclusions?'

His question drew a confused frown and he realised that she was too upset to focus on the facts.

She'd seen. She'd believed. She hadn't questioned. Hadn't cared enough to question and the knowledge that she hadn't cared left the bitter taste of failure in his mouth.

In a life gilded by success, she'd been his only failure.

Leandro flexed his shoulders to relieve the tension and the movement caught her attention, her eyes drifting to the swell of hard muscle. Her gaze was feather light and yet he felt the responding sizzle of sexual heat and almost laughed at his own weakness.

It seemed his body was nowhere near as choosy as his mind.

Millie stared at him for a long moment and then sank her teeth into her lower lip. 'Leandro, do me a favour.' Her voice was strained. 'Put your shirt on. We can't have a proper conversation with you standing there half-naked.'

'This may surprise you, but I've been known to conduct a conversation even when naked.' His sardonic tone masked his own anger and brought a flush to her cheeks.

'I'm sure. But if it's all the same with you, I'd like you to get dressed.'

'Why? Is the sight of my body bothering you, Millie?' His tone silky smooth, Leandro strolled across the bedroom and retrieved his shirt from the floor. 'Are you finding it hard to concentrate?' He shrugged the shirt back on, discovered that there were no buttons and spread his arms in an exaggerated gesture of apology. 'She was a bit over-eager, I'm afraid. This is the best I can do.'

'It's fine.' She averted her eyes, but not before both of them had shared a memory they would rather have forgotten. 'The media have been running the story for days now, and it's *awful*. Somehow they know about you and my sister, and they know the baby's been brought here.' Her voice wobbled. 'Where…?'

'Asleep on the next floor.' His voice terse, Leandro strolled over to the window that overlooked the garden. 'Someone from the clinic brought the baby to me. Your sister left him alone and uncared for while she went for her little drive. He was found crying and neglected.' The anger in him was like a roaring beast and he was shocked by the strength required to hold it back. Control was a skill he'd mastered at an impossibly young age, but when he thought of the baby his thoughts raced into the dark. 'Evidently she didn't have a maternal bone in her body.' *Another woman, another place.*

'She was sick.'

'Well, that's one thing we agree on.' *Infested with greed.* Aware that the past and the present had become dangerously tangled and the conversation was taking a dangerous turn, Leandro changed direction. 'Why do you think they brought the baby here, Millie?'

'The clinic said she left a note saying that you were the father. She wanted the baby to be with family.'

He made an impatient sound, marvelling at her naivety. 'Or perhaps she just wanted to make sure there was no chance of reconciliation between us. Her last, generous gift to you.' His carefully planted seed of suggestion landed on barren ground.

'There never was any chance of reconciliation.' She didn't look at him. 'Where's the baby? I should be going.'

Leandro stilled. 'Where, exactly, are you planning to go?'

'It's already past midnight. I've booked into a small bed and breakfast near here.'

'A bed and breakfast?' Leandro looked at her with a mixture of disbelief and fascination, realising just how little he knew about this woman. 'Are you suggesting what I think you are?'

'I'm taking the baby, of course. What did you think?'

'So you're planning to take in your sister's baby and care for it—this is the same baby that is supposedly the result of an affair between your own sister and your husband. Whether you think your sister was lying or telling the truth—'

'Telling the truth.'

Leandro's jaw tightened. 'Whichever. Your sister wrecked your marriage. She hurt you. And you're willing to take her baby? What are you, a doormat?'

Her narrow shoulders were rigid. 'No, I'm responsible. And principled. Qualities that you probably don't recognise. Am I angry with my sister? Yes, I'm angry. And that feels really horrible because even while I'm grieving I'm hurt that she could have done that to me.' Her voice shook. 'She behaved terribly. Some people wouldn't forgive that. If I'm honest I'm not sure that I'll ever forgive that. She betrayed my trust. But at least she was in love with you. And I think at the end she was truly sorry.'

Leandro raised an eyebrow but she ploughed on.

'It was the guilt that pushed her into depression. And whatever had happened, I would never have wanted her to…' Her voice trembled. 'We were sisters. And as for the baby— well, I don't believe that a child should be held responsible for the sins of his parents. My sister is dead. You can't bring up a baby, so I will have him. He will have a loving home with me as long as he needs one.'

'So you're proposing to love and care for your husband's bastard, is that right?'

'Don't *ever* call him that.' Her eyes blazed. 'And, yes, I'm intending to care for him. He's three months old. He's helpless.'

Curiously detached, Leandro looked at her. She wasn't classically beautiful, he mused, but there was something about her face that was captivating. 'So you have forgiven your sister.'

'I'm working on it.' She caught her lip between her teeth. 'I understand the effect you have on a woman. Even that Hollywood actress was willing to humiliate herself to spend a night with you. Tell me one thing—why, when you have a reputation for not committing to a woman, did you marry me?'

'Frankly?' Leandro lifted his eyes from his scrutiny of her soft lips. 'At this moment I have absolutely no idea.'

'You *really* know how to hurt. You treated our marriage lightly.'

'On the contrary, *you're* the one who walked out at the first obstacle.'

Her shoulders sagged, as if she was bearing an enormous weight. 'If you've said everything you wanted to say, I'd like to take the baby.'

'As usual you are being quite breathtakingly naïve. For a start there is a pack of journalists on my doorstep. How do you think they're going to react if you leave here clutching the baby?'

'I think it would reflect very badly on you. But you don't care about that, do you? You never care what people think about you. If you did, you wouldn't bchave so badly.'

Leandro pressed the tips of his long fingers to his forehead, his control at breaking point. 'We'll talk about this in a minute,' he snapped. 'For goodness' sake, go and use the bathroom. You're soaking wet. And next time use the front door, like my wife, instead of creeping through the garden like a burglar.'

'Whatever you say, you wouldn't have wanted those headlines any more than I did.'

Leandro sent her a brooding glance, marvelling that the male libido could be such a self-destructive force. 'The headlines will stop when they realise there is no story.'

She didn't appear to register his words. Certainly she didn't question his meaning. 'As soon as I'm dry, I'll take him away. We'll both be out of your life.'

Leandro watched in silence, allowing her to delude herself for a short time.

His wife was back.

And he had no intention of letting her walk out again.

CHAPTER TWO

NUMB with misery, Millie stood in front of the mirror in the huge, luxurious bathroom. She didn't reach for a towel. She did nothing to improve her appearance. She simply stared at herself.

No wonder, she thought numbly. *No wonder he'd strayed.*

Leandro Demetrios was six feet two inches of devastatingly handsome, vibrant masculinity and she was—she was, what?

Ordinary.

She was just so *ordinary.*

Staring at her wild, curling hair, she reflected on how long it had taken her each day to straighten it into the tame, sleek sheet that everyone expected. And even with the weight she'd lost during the misery of the last year, her breasts were still large, and her hips curvy.

No wonder he'd chosen her sister.

Trying not to think about that, Millie ran the tap and splashed cold water on her face. One thing about already having lost your husband to another woman, she thought, was that you no longer had to pretend to be someone different. She could just be herself. What did she have to lose?

Nothing.

She'd already lost it all.

But life kept throwing boulders at her, and she had a whole new challenge ahead of her. She had to put aside all her dreams of having her own baby, and instead love and nurture the baby that had been the result of her husband's affair with her sister.

Caught in a sudden rush of panic, Millie covered her mouth with her hand. It was all very well to say she was going to do this, but what if she looked at the baby and hated it? That would make her an awful person, wouldn't it?

She wanted to do the right thing, she really did, but what if doing the right thing proved too hard?

Her encounter with Leandro had been a million times harder than she'd anticipated and she'd always known it was going to be awful.

Even though their marriage was over, nothing had prepared her for the agonising pain of seeing Leandro with another woman. And worse still was the realisation that she hadn't healed at all. She wasn't over him and she never would be.

She'd learned to survive, that was all. But life without him was flat and colourless.

'Millie?' Leandro's harsh tones penetrated the closed door and she stilled, fastened to the spot like a rabbit caught in headlights. Then her eyes slid to the bolt on the door. Even Leandro in a black temper couldn't break his way through a solid bolt, could he?

She didn't understand his anger. Surely he should have been grateful to her for solving a problem for him. The last thing he needed in his life was a baby.

An image of the actress slid into her brain and paralysed her. For a moment she couldn't move or think.

What had she expected? That he was sitting in alone at night, thinking of her?

'Wait a minute!' Hands shaking, she looked at herself in the mirror, hoping that she'd turn out to be the person she hoped she was. She didn't want to be a pathetic, jealous wimp, did she? She wanted to have the strength to walk away from this marriage with her head held high and her dignity intact. She wanted to be mature enough to care for the baby and give him the love he deserved, regardless of how much his parents had hurt her.

That was the person she wanted to be.

Gritting her teeth, Millie turned away from the mirror, walked across the bathroom and opened the door.

Leandro was leaning against the doorframe, dark lights in his eyes warning her of just how short his fuse was. 'What have you been doing for the last half an hour? You look exactly the same as you did when you went in. I assumed you were going to shower and change. Or at least use a towel.'

Up until that point she hadn't realised that she'd forgotten to dry herself. 'I…didn't have anything to change into.'

Leandro reached out a hand and touched her damp hair with a frown of exasperation. 'You didn't bring any clothes.'

'I left my suitcase on the train,' she muttered. 'I was…upset. And I'm only staying in London for one night. It will be fine.' She wished she could feel angry again. The anger had given her energy to cope with the difficult situation. Without it, she felt nothing but exhaustion.

His hand dropped to his side. 'You still have clothes here. Wear them.'

'You kept my clothes?' Shocked, Millie stared up at him and his cold, unemotional appraisal chilled her.

'I hate waste and I find them useful for overnight guests.'

The barb sank deep, the pain resting alongside the earlier

wounds he'd inflicted, and she wondered why it was that emotional agony could be so much more traumatic than physical wounds.

He'd dismissed her from his life so easily.

Millie thought about all the bleak, lonely hours she'd spent agonising over whether or not she was right to have walked out—*about the tears she'd shed.* The times she'd wondered whether he was thinking about her. Whether he cared about their break-up.

Well, she had her answer now.

He was just fine. He'd moved on—apparently with effortless ease. Which just proved that he'd never loved her. He'd married her on impulse. He'd seen her as a novelty. Unfortunately it hadn't taken long for her novelty value to wear off. When they'd been living in their own little world everything had been fine. It had been when they'd returned to *his* world that the problems had started.

Did you really think you'd be able to hold him? Her sister's sympathetic question was embedded in her brain, like a soundtrack that refused to stop playing.

'The baby.' Knowing that the only way she was going to be able to hold it together was if she didn't dwell on how she felt, Millie forced herself to ask the question. 'Who has been looking after him?'

'Two nannies. Change your clothes,' Leandro said roughly. 'The last thing I need is you with pneumonia.'

'I'm not cold.'

'Then why are you shivering?'

Did he honestly not know? She wanted to hit him for not understanding her feelings. He possessed confidence by the barrel-load and that natural self-assurance seemed to prevent him understanding those to whom life didn't come quite so easily. What did a man like Leandro Demetrios know about insecurity? He didn't have a clue.

Neither had he shown any remorse for the way their relationship had ended. In fact, he'd made it obvious that he thought she'd been in the wrong.

Maybe other women would have turned a blind eye, but she wasn't like that.

'I'm shivering because I'm finding this situation…' She struggled to find a suitably neutral word. 'Difficult.'

'Difficult?' His sensual mouth formed a grim, taut line in his handsome face. 'You haven't begun to experience difficult yet, *agape mou*. But you will.'

What did he mean by that?

What could possibly be worse than being forced into the company of the man she adored and hadn't been able to satisfy, and forced to care for the child he'd had with another woman? At the moment that challenge felt like the very essence of difficulty.

Feeling as though she was balancing precariously on the edge of a deep, dark pit, Millie took a deep breath. 'I'd like to see my nephew.' She drew the edges of her damp cardigan around her. She was shivering so hard she might have been in the Arctic, rather than his warm bedroom. 'Where's the baby?'

'Sleeping. What else did you expect at this hour?' His mouth grim, he strode across the bedroom and into the dressing room, emerging moments later with some clothes in his hands. 'Put these on. At least they're dry.'

'They're my old jeans.' She frowned down at them. 'The ones I wore when I first met you.'

'This isn't a trip down memory lane,' he gritted. 'It's an attempt to get you out of wet clothes. Get back in that bathroom. And this time when you come out, make sure you're dry.'

With a sigh, Millie turned back into the bathroom. The lights came on automatically and she stopped, remembering how that had amused her when he'd first brought her to this house. She'd walked in and out of all the rooms, feeling as though she'd walked into a vision of the future. Lights that came on when someone walked into a room, heating sensors, a house that vacuumed itself—Leandro exploited cutting-edge technology in every aspect of his life, and for her it had been like walking into a fantasy.

Trying not to think how the fantasy had ended, Millie stripped off her wet clothes, rubbed her cold skin with a warm towel and pulled on the jeans and silky green jumper he'd handed her.

She glanced in the enormous mirror and decided that the lighting had been designed specifically to highlight her imperfections. She looked nothing like a billionaire's wife.

Emerging from the bathroom, her eyes clashed with his. 'Now can I see the baby? I just...' She swallowed. 'I just want to look at him, that's all.' *To get it over with. Part of her was so afraid she wouldn't be able to do it.*

This was a test, and she wasn't sure whether she was going to pass or fail.

Leandro yanked a towel from the rail and starting rubbing her hair. 'You've been in that bathroom twice and your hair is still soaking.'

'You need to invest in a device that automatically dries someone's hair if it's wet.'

Something flickered in his eyes and she knew he was thinking of the time when he'd first brought her here and she'd played with the technology like a child with a new toy. 'What were you doing all that time?'

Thinking about him. About her life.

Trying to find the strength to do this.

'I was playing hide and seek with the lights. They're a bit bright for me.' Millie winced as his methodical rubbing became a little too brisk and tried not to think about the fact that he was turning her hair into a tangled mess.

What did it matter? What did smooth, perfect hair matter at this point in their relationship? They were way past the point where her appearance was an issue.

Leandro slung the towel over the heated rail. 'That will do.'

'Yes, there's no point in working on something that's never going to come up to scratch,' Millie muttered, and he frowned sharply.

'What's that supposed to mean?'

'Nothing.' Trying to forget her appearance, Millie lifted her chin. 'I want to see the baby.' At least the baby wouldn't care whether her hair was blow-dried or not.

She felt inadequate and out of place in this man's life, but she was here because the baby needed her. It was abandoned. Unloved. *Like her…*

For a whole year she'd locked herself away—*protected herself from the outside world.* And if it hadn't been for the baby she would have stayed in her hiding place. Not that she'd needed to hide. *Leandro hadn't come to look for her, had he?* She'd left, but he hadn't followed.

Leandro gave her a long, hard look, as if asking himself a question.

Knowing with absolute certainty what that question was, Millie walked towards the bedroom door.

'You can see the baby,' he drawled as they walked out of the room. 'But don't wake him up.'

The comment surprised her. Why would he care whether

she woke the baby or not? She'd thought he would have been only too anxious for her to remove the child and get out of his life.

Millie glanced at the paintings, reflecting that most normal people had to go to art galleries to see pieces like this. Leandro could admire them on his way to the bathroom.

Following him up a flight of stairs, she frowned. 'You've put him as far away from you as possible.'

'You think he should sleep in my bedroom, perhaps?' His silken enquiry brought a flush to her cheeks.

'No. I don't think that. I can't think of a less suitable environment for a baby than your bedroom.'

Millie leaned against the wall for support, unable to dispel the image of his hard, muscular body entwined with the sylph-like actress.

Of course he'd had relationships since they'd broken up. What had she expected? Leandro was an intensely virile man with a dark, restless sex appeal that women found irresistible. Just as she had. And her sister.

Millie gave a low moan, wondering how she'd ever found the arrogance to think their marriage could work. How naïve had she been, thinking that they shared something special. When they'd first met he'd been so good at making her feel beautiful that for a while she'd actually believed that she was.

Leandro opened a door and stood there, allowing her to go first.

Her arm brushed against the hard muscle of his abdomen and her stomach reacted instantly.

A uniformed nanny rose quickly to her feet. 'He's been very unsettled, Mr Demetrios,' she said in a low voice. 'Crying, refusing his bottle. He's asleep now, but I don't know how long it will last.'

Leandro dismissed her with a single imperious movement of his head and the girl scurried out of the room.

Had he always been that scary? Millie wondered. *Had he been cold and intimidating when she'd met him?*

The answer was yes, probably, but never with her. With her he'd always been gentle and good humoured. That was one of the things that had made her feel special. The power and influence he wielded made others stutter and stumble around him, but when they'd met, she hadn't known who he was. And that had amused him. And she'd continued to amuse him. With *her,* the tiger had sheathed his claws and played gently, but she'd never been under any illusions. She hadn't tamed the tiger and she doubted any woman ever would.

As the door closed behind the girl, Millie wondered how on earth she'd ever had the courage to talk to this man.

'Your nephew.' He spoke the words in a low tone and Millie forced aside all other feelings and tiptoed towards the cot. Her palms were clammy and she felt ever so slightly sick because she'd pictured this scene in her head so many times, but now it was twisted in a cruel parody of her dream.

Yes, she and Leandro were leaning over a cot. But her dream had never included a baby who wasn't hers, fathered by the man she loved with the woman who was closest to her.

Agony ripped through her, stealing her breath and her strength. She thought she gave a moan of denial, but the baby didn't stir, his perfect features immobile in sleep.

Innocent of the tense atmosphere in the room, he was so still that Millie felt a rush of panic and instinctively reached out a hand to touch him.

Strong fingers closed over hers and drew her away from the cot.

'He's fine.' Leandro's low, masculine voice brushed

against her nerve endings. 'He always sleeps like that. *When* he sleeps, which isn't that often.'

'He looks—'

'As though he isn't breathing. I know.' He gave a grim smile. 'I've made that mistake several times myself. Once I even woke him up just to check he was alive. Believe me, I don't advise it. He's very much alive and if you poke him just to check, he'll confirm it in the loudest possible way. He has lungs that an opera singer would envy and, once woken up, he doesn't like going back to sleep. I had to walk him round the house for three hours.'

Leandro worried about the baby so much he'd woken him? And then he'd carried him around the house? It didn't fit with what she knew of him.

'What did you do with your BlackBerry?' She asked the question without thinking and he gave a faint smile.

'You think I spoke into the baby and tucked my mobile phone into the cot?' His eyes were mocking and Millie looked away, flustered.

'I didn't think you'd want anything to do with the baby.' In a way her question was a challenge. Would he care for a baby that wasn't his?

For a moment—*just for a moment*—something shimmered between them and then she dragged her eyes away from his and focused on the baby. Her heart was thumping, her stomach was tumbling over and over. But he'd always had this effect on her, hadn't he? He could turn her legs to jelly with just one glance. Everything else became irrelevant.

Except that it wasn't irrelevant and she had this baby to remind her of that fact.

He lay quietly. Even in sleep Millie could see the dark feathering of his eyelashes against his cheek and the shock of dark hair. And her heart melted. To her intense relief, the baby softened everything inside her. 'You poor thing,' she whispered, gently touching his head with her hand. 'You must be missing your mummy—wondering what you're doing in this strange place.' Aware that Leandro was looking at her oddly, she flushed. 'Sorry. I suppose it's a bit crazy speaking to a baby who's asleep.'

Her eyes met his and in that single instant she knew he was thinking about the child they could have made together. The image was too painful and she looked away, determined not to torture herself with what she would never have. *If she'd produced a child quickly, perhaps this would never have happened.* But that had been another failure on her part. Another failure to add to the list. 'He's sweet. He has your hair.'

'Then the child is a miracle of conception,' Leandro snapped. 'But I can assure you that your sister was definitely the mother.'

Millie struggled not to react. 'Becca was always confident. I think that's why she was so successful. It just didn't enter her head that she couldn't do something or have something.' *Even her sister's husband.* 'Like you, she never questioned herself or doubted herself. You had that in common.'

'Alpha woman.'

Millie looked at him. 'Yes. She was.' And she'd always felt insecure around her big sister. There had been just no way she could ever measure up. Even as a very young child, she'd been aware that she was walking in her sister's shadow.

And even in death Becca had left that shadow—a dark cloud that had stolen the light from Millie's marriage. *From her life.*

'Let's leave the baby to sleep.' Taking control, Leandro put a hand in the centre of her back and urged her out of the room. 'Have you eaten?'

'No.' Millie wondered how he could be thinking about food. 'It's past midnight. I was going to go straight to the bed and breakfast.'

'You're not going to any bed and breakfast. We need to talk— and I need coffee, so we'll have the conversation in the kitchen.'

Too drained to argue, Millie followed him downstairs. The kitchen was another room that had surprised her when she'd first seen the house. It was a clever combination of modern and traditional, a large range cooker giving warmth and comfort, while the maximal use of glass ensured light poured into every available space. As a result the lush garden appeared to be part of the room and the table was positioned in such a way that, whatever the season, it felt as though you were sitting outdoors.

'Sit down before you fall down.' Leandro strolled to the espresso machine and ground some beans.

The sound pounded her throbbing head and Millie winced. 'You still make it all from scratch, then?' It had been one of the many things that she'd learned about him early on. He wanted the best. Whether it was art, coffee or women— Leandro demanded perfection. *Which made it even more surprising that he'd picked her.*

He made the coffee—as competent in the kitchen as he was everywhere else. Leandro used staff because his life was so maniacally busy, not because he was deficient in skills. And sometimes, she knew, he just preferred to be on his own.

He'd rolled back his shirtsleeves and the muscles of his forearm flexed as he worked.

Strong, Millie thought as she looked at him. He was strong; physically, emotionally—and that inherent strength was part of his devastating appeal. He was a man who led while others followed. A man women were drawn to.

'Why didn't you tell me that the baby had been brought here?' To distract herself, she asked the question that was on her mind. 'Why did I have to read about it in the newspapers?'

'You walked out on me.' His voice terse, he reached for a cup. 'I had no reason to think you'd be interested.'

Absorbing that blow, Millie curled her fingers over the back of the chair. 'Why are you so angry with me? I would have thought you'd be apologetic or at least a little uncomfortable but you're not. You're…'

'I'm what, Millie?'

'You're…' She hesitated. 'Boiling with rage. And I just don't get it.'

He didn't reply, but she knew he'd heard her because his hand stilled for a moment. And then he lifted an empty cup. 'Do you want one?'

'No, thank you. You make it so strong it will keep me awake.' Not that she'd sleep anyway. The adrenaline was pumping round her bloodstream like a drug. She wanted to walk. Pace. *Sob?*

Leandro waited while the thick dark brew filled the small cup. Then he walked across to the table. 'Right, let's talk.' He put the cup on the table and sprawled in the nearest chair. The edges of his torn dress shirt slid apart, revealing his flat, bronzed abdomen.

Millie kept her eyes fixed straight ahead. 'What is there to talk about?'

'This is going to be a tiring conversation for you if you stand all the way through it. And you already look ready to drop.'

She sat, too emotionally wrung out to think for herself. 'I'm fine.'

'You look wrecked. You should have told me you were coming. I would have sent my private jet.'

'I wouldn't have felt comfortable.'

'You're still my wife. You're entitled to the perks of the job.'

'I don't want anything from you.' Millie sat very upright. 'Except maybe the stuff you've bought for the baby. It's a waste to buy a second pram and things. Tomorrow I'll remove Costas from your life. You can get back to your BlackBerry and your—' She almost said 'actress' but thought better of it. 'And your undisturbed nights.' From the corner of her eye she saw his fingers close round his coffee cup.

'I don't want to talk about Costas.' He let that hover in the air while he drank his coffee. 'I want to talk about us.'

Her heart started to thump faster because she could feel him watching her and his scrutiny made her squirm. 'How is that relevant?'

'It's relevant.'

'How? There is no "us". There's nothing to talk about.' Why would he want to go back over old ground? Millie wasn't sure she could stand reliving the whole thing again.

'You made promises, Millie. You stood up in that little village church and made those vows.' Leandro put his cup down slowly. 'And then you just walked away. *For richer for poorer, in sickness and in health*—remember that?'

Her chin lifted. *'Forsaking all others…'*

'I might have known you'd throw that one at me.' He inhaled deeply, his eyes holding hers. 'You asked me how it's relevant—let me tell you. You're my wife, Millie. And to a Greek man, marriage is binding. It isn't something you opt in and out of depending on the mood. It's forever.'

'Leandro—'

'You chose to come back, Millie.' His mouth tightened and his eyes glinted hard and dangerous. 'And now you're going to stay.'

CHAPTER THREE

MILLIE sat in frozen silence, so stunned by his unexpected declaration that she could barely breathe, let alone speak. It took several uncomfortable moments for the full implications of his words to sink into her shocked brain.

Then she sprang to her feet and paced to the far side of the kitchen, so agitated that it was impossible to stay still. 'You expect me to come back to you? You're blaming me for walking away?'

'Yes.' His tone was hard. 'I am.'

Millie stared at the row of shiny saucepans on the wall. 'The fact that you won't let me take the baby tells me only one thing.'

Leandro gave a humourless laugh. 'I always insist that my employees are capable of thinking laterally. For some reason I didn't apply the same standards to my wife. Take a word of advice from me—when you study a picture, there is almost always more going on than first meets the eye.'

'I can see only one reason why you'd be so protective of this baby.'

'Then remind me not to set you up in business. Tunnel vision is a guaranteed path to failure.' He was a tough adversary—intelligent, articulate and able to counter every word spoken with the effortless ease of a practised negotiator. 'Did you really think I'd let you walk out with him? A baby is a massive responsibility, requiring the ultimate commitment. Given your track record, I'm hardly likely to hand him over.'

'*My* track record?'

'When you met an obstacle in life, you walked away.'

His accusation was so unfair that her breath hitched. 'You were with my sister. What did you expect? My blessing?'

'You are my wife. I expected your trust.' He was on his feet, too. And determined to halt her retreat. 'Answer me a question.' His handsome face taut and grim, he closed his hands over her shoulders. 'After everything we shared—after those vows you made—why were you so quick to believe the worst of me? You stalked out that night and you never contacted me again. You didn't ask me about it.'

Her eyes level with his bare chest, Millie's heart was pounding uncomfortably. 'I saw what I saw.'

'You saw what your sister wanted you to see.'

'I know that some of the blame lay with her, but—'

'Not some of it,' his tone was harsh, 'all of it. She set you up, Millie, and you believed all the lies she fed you. And I was so angry that you believed her, I let you go. And that was a mistake, I admit that. One of many I've made where you're concerned. I should have run after you, pinned you to our bed and made you see the truth.'

'Don't do this!' Millie covered her ears with her hands. 'Why are you doing this now when it's all too late?'

'Because this is a conversation we need to have. What about those feelings you claimed you had for me, Millie? Or was it all a damn lie because you wanted the lifestyle?'

She almost laughed at that. The lifestyle had been the

problem, but he'd never understand that, would he? 'I didn't care about the lifestyle.'

'Really? For a woman who didn't care, you certainly spent enough time on your appearance.'

It was such an unexpected interpretation of the facts that for a moment Millie just gaped at him. *He had no idea.* 'What you said just now,' she croaked, 'about a picture sometimes having another meaning—'

'Shopping is shopping.' There was an acid bite to his tone. 'It's hard to find another meaning for that. Unless you convinced yourself that it was an act of charity to prop up the world economy single-handed.'

Millie was so shocked and stung by that all she managed by way of response was a little shake of her head. 'I was trying to be the woman you wanted me to be.'

'What the hell is that supposed to mean?'

Wasn't it obvious? She was standing in front of him in her oldest jeans with bubbling hair and no make-up. The shiny surface of his large American fridge reflected her deficiencies back at her. Even in the kitchen there was no escape. 'I'm not your type. We met and married in less than a month. It was just too quick. We didn't know each other. It was a mistake.'

'Which part, exactly, was the mistake?' He made a rough sound in his throat and stepped towards her, trapping her against the wall with the sheer force of his presence. 'The part when you lay underneath me, sobbing my name?'

She felt the hard muscle of his thighs against her. 'Leandro—'

He slid his hand into her hair, tilting her face so that she was forced to look at him. 'Or the part when you came again and again without any break in between—was that when you thought, This is a mistake?'

'Don't do this—please don't do this.' Millie pushed at his chest and immediately regretted it because her hands encountered sleek muscle and it took every fibre of her being not to slide her greedy fingers over the deliciously masculine contours of his chest.

'When you fell asleep with your head on my shoulder, were you dreaming of mistakes?'

He'd conjured up one of her most precious memories and she closed her eyes against the tears and felt them scald the backs of her eyelids. The sex had always been incredible but also a little bit overwhelming because she could never quite let go of the thought that a man like him couldn't possibly want a girl like her. But in those moments afterwards—*those moments when he'd held her and murmured soft words against her hair*—that had been her favourite time. The time she'd actually let herself believe that the fairy-tale might be happening.

'When you told me that you loved me, Millie…' His voice was hoarse and his fingers tightened in her hair. 'Were you thinking that it was a mistake? Was it all a lie?'

'No.'

Her eyes flew to his and for one desperate moment she thought he might actually kiss her. His mouth hovered, a muscle flickered in his lean, dark jaw and his eyes glittered black and dangerous. He looked like a man on the edge.

And then he stepped back from the edge, displaying that formidable control that raised him apart from other men. 'I don't think you know what you want, Millie. And that's why I'm not letting you take this baby.' With a searing glance in her direction, he closed his hand over her wrist and propelled her back to the table. 'Sit down.'

'Leandro, you can't—'

'I said *sit down*. I haven't finished.' His harsh tone was all the more shocking because she'd never heard it before. Always, with her, he'd been gentle. She'd never been on the receiving end of his biting sarcasm or his brutal frankness.

'If you yell, I won't listen.'

'I'm *not* yelling.' But he drew in a breath to calm himself and Millie sat, wondering again why he was so angry.

'Leandro—'

'You walked out without even giving me a hearing,' he said thickly, 'and at the time I was so angry with you that I let you go. Your lack of trust diminished what we shared to nothing. But I can see how skilfully your sister manipulated you. I can almost understand why you might have believed what you believed. You're right. We didn't know each other well enough or you wouldn't have run so fast. You wouldn't have looked at me with that accusation in your eyes. You wouldn't have been so quick to doubt me. You would have known me better.'

'I saw you,' she whispered, but his gaze didn't waver.

'What did you see, Millie? You saw your sister naked in the pool with me. Isn't that what you saw?'

The reminder was like the sting of a whip. 'You're trying to tell me I was imagining things.'

'No. I'm trying to make you see the rest of the picture. Was *I* naked?' His tone demanded an answer. 'Was I having sex with her?'

'Not then, no, but—'

'Can you think of any other reasons why Becca might have been naked in my pool?'

'Frankly, no.' Millie wished he'd sit down too. Staring up at six feet two of muscle-packed male wasn't an experience designed to induce relaxation.

Her answer drew a frustrated growl from him and he

muttered something under his breath in Greek. 'Perhaps your sister wasn't quite the person you thought she was.'

'It isn't fair to talk about her like this when she's not here to defend herself!'

'Fair?' His voice exploded with passion. 'Don't talk to me about fair!'

'You blame my sister, but you're no saint, Leandro.'

He gave a twisted smile. 'I have never laid claim to that title.'

'You have a dangerous reputation. Before me you'd dated all those beautiful women and you hadn't committed to any of them.' Millie bit her lip, wondering how she could have been such a fool.

'And what does that tell you?'

'It tells me that you're not good at sticking with one person.'

Tension vibrating through his powerful frame, Leandro stared up at the ceiling, apparently trying to control his response. When he finally looked at her again, his eyes glinted volcanic black and his body language was forceful and menacing as he loomed over her.

'Given that you can only see one image, I am going to have to show you the rest of the picture. But I'm only going to say this once,' he said softly, 'so make sure you are listening.'

'*Stop* trying to intimidate me.'

Shock shimmered in his eyes and his head jerked back as if she'd slapped him. 'I am *not* intimidating you.'

'That depends on where you're sitting.' Her voice was strong and steady and Millie had the satisfaction of seeing him take a deep breath.

Inclining his head by way of apology, he modulated the tone of his voice. 'Understand that the only reason I'm prepared to give you this explanation is because you're my wife and that allows you a degree of leeway that I would *never* grant to another person.'

Millie wanted to point out that she didn't inhabit that role any more but she couldn't push the words past her dry throat.

'Millie—look at me.'

She looked.

'I did *not* have sex with your sister.' Leandro spoke the words with deadly emphasis. 'At no time in our short, ill-fated marriage was I ever unfaithful to you. The baby is not mine.'

Millie's heart jumped. *She wanted to believe*—and then she remembered her sister. 'Why would Becca lie?' She breathed in and out. 'That would make her…'

Leandro straightened, his expression cold. 'Yes,' he said flatly, 'it would.'

'I know what I saw.'

'I've given you the facts. You decide. I have never doubted your intelligence, just your ability to use it.'

Millie stared at him in confusion, thinking of what he'd just said. *What she'd seen.* Everything she knew, everything she'd believed was suddenly thrown in the air. It was as if someone had dropped a giant jigsaw puzzle and the picture was no longer visible. 'One of you is—was—lying,' she said hoarsely, and he gave a grim smile.

'And your sister is no longer able to tell you the truth. An interesting dilemma, *agape mou*. Who are you going to believe? Live husband, or dead sister?'

Faced with that choice, her head started to throb. 'Let me tell you about my sister, Leandro. Let me tell you what my sister was to me. It was Becca who held my hand on my first day at school. It was Becca who helped me with my maths homework. It was Becca who taught me how to do my hair and make-up. Every step of my life, she was there, *helping* me. She encouraged me when my parents barely noticed I existed. It's bad enough to think she'd have an affair with my husband, but now you're suggesting she made up this entire thing just to hurt me?'

His silence said more than a thousand words would have done and Millie gave a distressed sigh.

'Obviously that *is* what you're suggesting. That's madness. What could she have possibly gained by that? And why would you expect me to believe you without question? I've known you a fraction of the time I knew my sister.'

'I expect you to believe me,' he said acidly, 'because you're my wife and that role should bring with it trust and commitment, two qualities that appear to be sadly lacking in your make-up. The truth is that our marriage started to go wrong long before you saw me with your sister.' Leandro straightened. 'I presume that's why you started avoiding sex.'

Her face flamed. 'I wasn't…avoiding sex.'

'Night after night you turned your back on me. You pretended to be asleep. And if I arrived home too early for you to play that trick, then you threw excuse after excuse at me—"headache", "tired", "wrong time of the month"—and I let you hold back because I was only too aware that you'd had absolutely no sexual experience before I came into your life. I was extremely patient with you. I had no idea what was going on in your head and you gave me no clues. You just lay there and hoped it would go away.'

The fact that he'd seen through her pitiful attempts to keep him at a distance increased her humiliation. 'I'm sure you really regretted marrying me.' *In fact, she knew he did. Wasn't that why he'd slept with her sister?*

'Do you want to know what I regret, Millie?' His voice was suddenly weary and he ran his hand over the back of his neck to relieve the tension. 'I regret that I didn't tie you to that damn bed and force you to tell me what was going on in that pretty head of yours. I backed off when I should have pushed you for answers, and I regret that more deeply than you'll ever know.'

'There was nothing in my head,' she lied. 'I was tired, that was all. When you weren't away on business trips, we were always out—every night there was something you wanted me to go to.' *Another event designed to highlight the differences between them and sap her confidence.*

'Tired?' His gaze was sardonic. 'On our honeymoon you had no sleep at all. We had sex virtually every hour of every day. You were as insatiable as I was. Fatigue wasn't the reason you had your back to me when I came to bed.'

'Leandro—'

'The honeymoon was perfect. The problems started when we arrived home. Suddenly you couldn't bear me to touch you. In fact, you went to the most extraordinary lengths to make sure that I didn't touch you.' His lips tightened. 'I even wondered whether the reason you invited your sister to stay with us was because you wanted something else to keep us apart.'

Appalled by the gulf in their mutual understanding, she dug her fingers into her hair and shook her head. 'You think I *wanted* you to have an affair with my sister?'

'I've said all I'm going to say on that particular subject.'

Millie was shaking so much she was relieved she was sitting down. 'I invited my sister to stay because I trusted her. And because I needed her help—she was always the one I turned to when I was in trouble.'

His brows met in a frown. 'How were you in trouble?'

Millie sat in silence, wishing she'd phrased it differently. Talking to him wasn't easy, was it? They didn't have that depth of understanding in their relationship. They'd shared scalding passion and nothing more. And Leandro was so confident, he wouldn't be able to understand anyone who wasn't. 'This is very hard for me,' she muttered, emotion swamping her. 'I didn't just lose my husband, I lost my sister. She was my best friend. And I lost her long before she died on that dusty, lonely road.'

'I want to know why you were so quick to assume that I'd have an affair. We'd been married three months, Millie! *Three months*. Hardly enough time for disillusionment to set in.'

'I knew your reputation.'

'Which was earned *before* I met you.'

Millie smiled through tears that refused to be contained. 'Oh, sure.' Her voice was choked. 'Beautiful me. So vastly superior in every way to those skinny models and actresses who knew how to dress, how to walk—I can quite see how it would have been impossible to notice them with me in the room. You should have reprogrammed the lights in this house so that they went *off* when I walked into a room. That might have helped our marriage.'

'Sarcasm doesn't suit you. It was your sweet nature and your gentleness that drew me to you.' Leandro's eyes narrowed, his gaze suddenly intent and focused. 'You always put yourself down. Why didn't I notice that before?'

'I don't know. At the beginning we didn't do much talking and after that you were too busy being exasperated with me for getting everything wrong, I suppose.' Millie thought about all those tense hours she'd spent trying to be who he wanted her to be. What an utter waste of time. Obviously she hadn't even come close. Which just proved that even eight hours in a beauty salon couldn't make a billionaire's wife out of a farm girl. 'You were partly to blame—you just dumped me in that situation and left me.'

'What situation?' He looked genuinely perplexed and she decided that there was no reason not to talk about it now.

It wasn't as if she was trying to impress him. She'd given up on that. 'You dumped me at all those really glitzy parties.'

'I did *not* "dump" you. I was by your side.'

'You were either talking business with someone in a suit— or you were smiling your smile at some beauty who was determined to grab your attention even though you were with me. And they all looked at me as though I'd crawled out from under a rock.'

'You were my wife.'

'Yes. That was the problem.'

Leandro gave her a look of exasperation. 'You are making no sense at all! Being my wife gave you status—'

'It was hugely stressful.'

He rubbed his fingers over his forehead. 'If this is a problem you expect me to discuss rationally, you're going to have to be a little more specific. In what way was being my wife "stressful"?'

Millie rubbed her hands over her legs, staring down at nails that had been bitten to nothing over the past year. 'I didn't have the necessary qualifications. I don't know why you married me, but you made a mistake.'

'Yes, you're right. I did make a mistake.' His fingers drummed a slow, deadly rhythm on the table. 'And I'm putting that mistake right and we're ending this mess.'

His words crushed her. For a horrible moment she thought she might make a fool of herself and slide to the floor and beg, *No, no, no.* The pride was stripped from her, leaving her vulnerable and exposed. She felt like a mortally wounded animal waiting for the final blow.

Oddly enough, the desire to cry suddenly ceased. It was as if her body had shut down.

'You want a divorce.' Somehow she managed to say the words, her eyes fixed on the wooden table, studying the grain of the wood. Anything, rather than look at him and fall apart. It was illogical, she knew, but she'd rather be married to him and never see him than cut the ties forever. 'Of course you do. Just let me take the baby, and I'll give you a divorce.'

'*Theos mou,* haven't you been listening to a word I've said?' His voice was rough and angry. 'I do *not* want a divorce.'

'You said you made a mistake.'

'It seems that whatever one of us says, the other misinterprets it.' Clearly struggling with his own volatile emotions, Leandro paused for a moment, his hand to his forehead. The he looked at her. 'The mistake I made,' he said harshly, 'was letting you walk out that day. I should have dragged you back and made you look at the truth. But I was furious that you doubted me. I was furious that you didn't stand your ground and fight for what we had.'

'If something isn't right, sometimes it's better just to let it go.'

Leandro threw her a fulminating glare and then paced to the far side of the kitchen, his broad shoulders rigid with tension.

Millie watched him—*this man she loved*—wondering what was going through his mind. As if reading her thoughts, he turned. The ever-present chemistry flickered across the room, resurrecting a connection that had never died.

'When I said that I'm ending this mess, I meant that we're ending this ridiculous separation. I want you back by my side where you belong. When the going gets tough, I want you to stay and fight instead of running. Those are the qualities I expect in the woman I've chosen to be my wife and the mother of my children.'

Millie pressed the palm of her hand against her heart to relieve the almost intolerable ache. 'Are you saying that you don't think I'd make a good mother?'

Something dark and dangerous shifted in his eyes. 'Let's just say that at the moment I'm not convinced.'

Appalled that he could possibly think that of her, Millie stared at him, seeing dark shadows in his eyes that she didn't understand. 'You don't know me at all.'

'No,' he said grimly. 'I don't. But I intend to rectify that.' He spoke the word with deadly emphasis. 'Let's see how powerful that commitment is this time around, shall we, Millie? If you want to be a mother to that child, you'll do it by my side, as my wife.'

The shock of his words silenced her and he lifted an eyebrow.

'It's a yes or no answer, Millie.'

She stood up, so agitated that she couldn't stay sitting. The fact that he intended to keep the baby suggested that he must be the father. Did he expect her to just ignore that fact? She wondered why he was so determined to continue the marriage. Was it a matter of pride? 'Why do you want this?' Her chair scraped on the floor, the sound grating against her jagged nerves. 'I don't understand you.'

'I know that. But you will have the whole of our marriage to understand me. And I'm going to understand you.' He strolled across to her and she stepped backwards, but he kept coming, backing her against the wall, planting his hands either side of her head. 'You and me, Millie.' His voice was suddenly dangerously masculine and she caught her breath because he was casting the same spell that had drawn her in right at the beginning.

'Leandro, don't—'

His hand caught her face, his gaze intense. 'I want you to stand by those promises you made to me in the church that day.'

His eyes darkened to a fierce black, as if her silence had somehow given him an answer to a question still unasked.

'Millie?'

Millie closed her eyes. She wanted to ask why he was so determined to keep the baby. Couldn't he see how that looked? Her mind was a mess—her thoughts so tangled and confused that she couldn't follow a single strand through to its conclusion. 'You can't just resurrect our marriage. We were a disaster.'

'Our communication was a disaster, that I agree.' Leandro shrugged. 'I rarely make mistakes and when I do, it's just once, so you can relax.'

She'd never felt less relaxed in her life. 'I can't be what you want me to be.'

Leandro gave a humourless laugh. 'Our communication has been so appalling up until this point, *agape mou,* I seriously doubt that you have any idea what I want from you. But this time around you will *not* be turning your back on me. And you will not be walking out when we hit a problem.'

Millie thought about what she had to offer him. *Even less than last time.* 'You want me to come back as your wife, but things have changed, Leandro. You don't know everything. Things have happened over the past year.'

'I don't want to know,' he said roughly, and she realised that he thought she was referring to another relationship.

'There are things I need to tell you.'

'Don't tell me. At least, not right now. I'm Greek, remember? I'm trying to be modern, but I have a long way to go.' With a low growl of frustration he lowered his head towards hers, the gesture an erotic reminder of everything they'd shared. For a moment his mouth hovered and he was obviously deciding whether to kiss her or not and then he lifted his head and stepped back. 'No. This time we're *not* going to let the sex do the talking. You look exhausted. Get some sleep. Just for tonight you can sleep in one of the spare bedrooms but after that you'll sleep where my wife is supposed to sleep. By my side.'

CHAPTER FOUR

'DON'T cry. Don't cry.' Crying herself, Millie held the baby against her, rocking gently as he gulped and sobbed.

She'd been lying fully dressed and wide awake on top of the bed in one of the rooms just down the corridor from the nursery when she'd heard the baby howling. Instantly she'd sprung from the bed, driven by a deep instinct that she hadn't felt before.

To begin with she'd stood back and allowed the nannies to comfort him, reminding herself that they were familiar to him, whereas she was a stranger. But after a few minutes she'd realised that they were getting nowhere and she'd taken over and dismissed them.

'Are you hungry? Is that what's wrong?' Wiping away her own tears on her sleeve, Millie lifted the baby out of the cot, feeling his sturdy body beneath her hands as she held him awkwardly. 'I haven't done this before so you'll have to tell me if I'm getting it wrong. Are you missing your mummy?' Although, from what the clinic had told her, Becca had spent precious little time with her baby.

The baby's yells increased and Millie settled herself in the chair and tentatively offered him the bottle that the nannies had left. 'Is this the right angle? I've never fed a baby before so you're going to have to yell a bit louder if I get it wrong.'

But the baby clamped his little mouth round the teat and sucked fiercely, gulping noisily as he greedily devoured the milk.

Millie gave an astonished laugh. 'You really are starving. You certainly don't take after your mother. She never ate anything.' As the baby fed, she stared down at him, examining his features with an agonising pang.

There was no escaping the fact that he had Leandro's hair. And his beautiful olive skin.

'Is he your daddy?' Speaking softly, she adjusted the angle of the bottle. 'And if he is, how do I live with that? I don't know. This is like one of those hypothetical dilemmas you talk about with your friends over a coffee. What would you do if your husband has an affair? Except maybe he didn't—I don't know. Should I really trust his word—or my sister's? Am I supposed to just overlook it? Is that what he means about being the wife of a Greek man? I'm supposed to be in the kitchen stirring a casserole while he's off having fun with his mistress?' The baby sucked rhythmically, his eyes fixed on her face. 'There's no way we can carry on where we left off, even if I wanted to. Everything has changed. Things happened to me—things he doesn't know about. He's assuming everything is the same as when I left, and it isn't.'

The baby sucked happily and Millie gave a watery smile. 'You're not giving me much help, are you? I don't know what to do. If I wasn't attractive enough to keep him the first time, it's going to be even worse this time. He doesn't know what he's taking on.' She thought about the last year and gave a despairing laugh. 'On the other hand, there's no way I'm leaving you here with him. You'll be corrupted in a month.'

One of the nannies appeared in the doorway. 'You persuaded him to take a bottle! We couldn't get him to feed. I'd really had it with him by the time I went off duty last night.' She yawned. 'I even woke Erica because she's been doing this job for twenty years and knows every trick in the book. But he wouldn't take it for her either. He's the most miserable baby we've ever looked after. Probably knows there's this big row about his parentage. His mum's dead, apparently. And sexy Leandro Demetrios is supposedly his father. Scandal, scandal, scandal.' She gave a conspiratorial giggle, and walked across the room. 'Of course, *he* won't say whether the baby is his or not, but he's taken it in, hasn't he? So that must say a lot.'

'It says that he's a responsible human being,' Millie said stiffly, concentrating on the baby and *hating* the thought that everyone was gossiping. 'Am I giving it to him too fast?'

'No. He's fine. He's not crying, is he? I much prefer toddlers. At least you have the option of sticking them in front of the television when you get fed up with them.' The nanny frowned. 'Thank goodness you've got the touch. I was expecting to get fired this morning.'

'Fired?'

The girl gave a fatalistic shrug. 'Well, Leandro Demetrios isn't exactly known as someone who accepts failure, is he? Erica and I decided in the night that if we hadn't got the baby to take the bottle by morning, both of us would be for the chop. Shame. The pay is good and the boss is gorgeous. We're trying to find excuses to be on his floor of the house in case he sleeps in the nude. So—who are you, exactly? I didn't know he was hiring anyone else.'

'I'm his wife.' The moment she'd said the words, Millie wished they could be unsaid because the girl gaped at her in astonished disbelief.

Then the drive for job security overtook her natural astonishment and she cleared her throat. 'I had no idea.' Her eyes slid from Millie's tumbling hair to her old jeans. 'God—sorry. I mean— And you're looking after his—' Her face turned scarlet but it was obvious from the look in her eyes that she thought Millie was a fool. 'We didn't know he was still married.'

'We've been apart for a while.'

'I see.' The girl's expression said, No wonder, and Millie wished she didn't mind so much. She *knew* she was an unlikely choice. Why did it still hurt so much to see the surprise in people's eyes? Why did she have to be so sensitive? Annoyed with herself for caring, she wished she were more like Leandro, who was always coolly indifferent to the opinions of everyone around him. Or failing that, she would have chosen to be more like Becca, who had been born assuming that the whole world adored her.

Would she have been more confident if she hadn't had Becca as an older sister? Or if she'd been born with Becca's blonde, perfect looks? Becca had appeared on the covers of all the high-class glossy magazines—her trademark slanting blue eyes and flirtatious expression guaranteeing the publication flew off the shelves.

'So…' The nanny looked at her curiously. 'Are the two of you back together, then?'

Were they?

The question was cheeky, but Millie had been asking herself the same thing all night. Instead of snatching some much-needed sleep, she'd locked herself in one of Leandro's many spare guest suites and lain on the bed, wondering whether she had the courage to face what was ahead of her if she agreed to his suggestion.

He'd reject her again, of course. Once he knew…

If she'd disappointed him then, how much more disappointed was he going to be this time?

But if she refused, she'd lose access to her sister's child. Her nephew.

As confused as ever, Millie carefully removed the teat from the baby's mouth. His stomach pleasantly full, he blinked his eyes and focused on her. And then he smiled. A lopsided, not very confident smile, but a smile nevertheless, and the nanny gave a short laugh.

'He's never done that before. He's never smiled at anyone. Can I have a cuddle?' She scooped the baby from Millie's arms and the baby's eyes flew wide and then his face crumpled. 'Oh, gosh, forget it.' Pulling an exasperated face, the nanny lowered the baby back into Millie's arms.

Costas immediately snuggled close and fell asleep.

The nanny rolled her eyes. 'Well, now you're stuck,' she said dryly. 'If you move, he'll wake up.'

'I don't need to move. I'll just stay here with him.'

'You're just going to sit holding him? That will get him into bad habits.'

'Since when is enjoying a cuddle a bad habit?'

'When it stops him wanting to sleep in his cot. You should put him in there and let him cry,' the nanny advised firmly. 'Let him know who's boss. It's five o'clock in the morning. Don't you want to go back to bed?'

To do what? Lie awake, thinking? Going over and over everything in her mind? She could do that here, cuddling the cause of her dilemma. 'I'm fine here.'

And she thought she *was* fine until the door opened and Leandro strode into the room.

'Oh!' The nanny flushed scarlet and gave an embarrassed laugh, the way women often did when they laid eyes on

Leandro Demetrios. Then she tweaked her uniform and smoothed her hair. Millie didn't blame her. Women did that too, didn't they? She'd tweaked her uniform and smoothed her hair every minute of every day they'd been together. The only difference being that her 'uniform' had been the designer clothes he'd bought her. Not that any of them had helped. The truth was that no amount of straightening and smoothing had transformed her into something that had looked good alongside his extraordinary looks.

Last night he'd been very much the dominant husband but this morning he was all billionaire tycoon. Smooth, sleek, expensive and indecently handsome. Everything about him shrieked of success in a realm above the reach of ordinary mortals, and Millie took one glance at the elegant dark grey suit and knew that he was off on one of his business trips.

'I need to talk to you before I leave for my meeting.' He turned and delivered a pointed glance at the nanny, who took the hint and melted away, closing the door behind her.

Millie was willing to bet she was standing outside it with her ear pressed to the wood. 'She has to go.'

In the process of looking at the baby, Leandro frowned. 'Go where?'

'Just go. The nanny. I don't want her looking after the baby.' Millie curved the baby against her and fiddled with the blanket that covered him. 'She's a gossip and her only interest in Costas is that his mother is dead and his father is a billionaire.'

'Whoever I appoint can't fail to be aware of the rumours surrounding this baby.'

'I agree, but she showed no warmth or care towards him. And she doesn't even *like* babies—she said she prefers them older. And even then she just sticks them in front of the television.'

'Fine.' He glanced at his watch. 'You want me to fire her, I'll fire her.'

'No. I'll do it,' Millie said firmly, and he lifted his eyebrows.

'*You?*'

'Yes.'

Leandro gave a disbelieving laugh. 'I'm seeing a totally different side to you today. I wouldn't have thought you were capable of firing someone.'

'It depends on the provocation. I'm thinking of Costas and what he needs. He doesn't need someone who is going to think about his parentage all the time. He needs someone who *likes* him.' She scanned Leandro's immaculate appearance. 'It's five in the morning. I can't believe you have a meeting at this hour.'

'I have a breakfast meeting at my offices in Paris. My pilot is waiting.'

'Of course he is.' Millie gave a weary smile. Other people queued for a bus. Leandro had a pilot waiting for his instructions. It was a reminder of how different their lives were. His house contained a pool, a spa, a media room and an underground garage complete with car lift, and *everything* was automated.

Millie thought of the tiny flat she'd been renting since she'd walked out a year earlier. If she wanted light, she had to press a switch, and even then it didn't always work because the electrics were so dodgy.

Leandro was frowning impatiently. 'Why was the baby crying?'

'I don't know. He hasn't had a good night. And neither of the nannies you appointed could get him to take the bottle. And having met one of them, I'm not surprised.'

'They have impressive references.'

'From whom?' Millie put the empty bottle down. 'Not the babies they looked after, I'm sure.'

His eyes narrowed. 'Delivering smart remarks seems to have become a new hobby of yours.'

Realising that for once she hadn't felt too intimidated to say what she thought, Millie gave a little smile. 'It wasn't a smart remark. It was the truth. I'm simply pointing out that what pleases a mother or an agency might not please a baby. This nursery is immaculate—everything in order—but they obviously haven't done anything to build a relationship with Costas.' She curved her nephew closer, lowering her voice. 'He was very upset. But he's settled down now. I think he was hungry.'

'The nannies weren't capable of giving him a bottle?'

'He wouldn't take it from them.'

'He seems to be taking it from you.'

'Perhaps he knows I'm on his side.'

'Perhaps.' He gave her a curious look, watching her with the baby, and she looked at him questioningly.

'Why are you staring? Do you want to hold him or something?'

'Not at the moment.'

'Of course. Sorry.' Millie flushed. 'I'm sure your suit cost a fortune. Baby sick on designer menswear isn't a good look.'

Leandro strolled over to her. 'I have more important things to worry about than the state of my suit. I do, however, care about disturbing an otherwise contented baby when I want a conversation. He's clearly comfortable with you at the moment and I'm wise enough to leave him where he is. If I take him, he'll protest, and neither of us will be able to talk.'

As if to signify his agreement, Costas nestled close to her, practised his smile again and then his eyes drifted shut.

Millie felt a warm feeling pass through her and a fierce stab of protectiveness.

'There's nothing to talk about. You're not the right man to look after a baby. You spent the first thirty-two years of your life avoiding babies. He needs someone who is going to forget the questions about his parentage and just love him.'

'And that's you?' Leandro studied her for a moment, incredulity lighting his dark eyes. 'Unless I'm misreading your extraordinarily expressive face, you still believe this baby to be the child of your husband and his lover.'

'That isn't relevant.'

'Most people would consider it relevant, Millie.' With a sardonic lift of his eyebrow, he studied her and then shrugged. 'Make whatever decisions you like about hiring and firing,' he said smoothly. 'Appoint whoever you want, but I do want him to have a nanny. You can care for him if you're willing to do that, but not at the expense of our relationship.'

Millie licked her lips. 'We still have to talk about that part.'

'Then talk. You had plenty to say for yourself a moment ago so don't expect me to believe you're suddenly short of opinions.' Leandro glanced at the Rolex on his wrist. 'Are you staying or going?'

It was her turn to look incredulous. 'How can you be so emotionally detached about the whole thing? This is our *marriage* you're talking about, not a corporate takeover. But I get the feeling I'm just another task on your ridiculously long "action" list! "Find out if Millie is staying or going."' She mimicked his voice. '"Tick that box."'

He gave a faint smile. 'You've changed.'

'Well, I'm sorry, but—'

'Don't apologise,' he drawled. 'I like it. If you're going to speak your mind, I might have a chance of knowing what's going on inside it. Why didn't you ever do this before?'

'Because you're scary.'

Leandro sucked in a breath and looked at her in genuine amazement. 'Scary? What do you mean, *scary?* I have never threatened you in any way.'

'It's not what you say or what you do, it's just who you are—' She broke off. 'I don't know. It isn't easy to describe. But next time you're being really scary I'll point it out.'

'Thank you.' The irony in his tone wasn't lost on her and she looked up at him, wishing he wasn't so insanely good-looking. Every time she looked at him she lost the thread of the conversation. It made it worse that she knew exactly what was underneath that sleek designer suit.

'All right. Let's get this over with. You want to know my decision, but it isn't that easy.' She glanced down at Costas, now sleeping quietly in her arms. 'I need some time to think about it.'

He leaned against the wall, tall handsome and breathtakingly confident. 'I've given you time.'

'I want *more* time.'

'You're my wife. What is there to think about?'

Millie adjusted the blanket. 'Whether or not it can work.'

'If you come back to this marriage expecting us to fall at the first fence, we'll fall.'

Millie thought about what he didn't know. 'Things have changed, Leandro.'

'Good. They needed to change.' He studied her thoughtfully, his gaze sharp. 'Did you find me scary in bed?'

'Sorry?' Her face burned but he refused to let her look away.

'You said you found me scary,' he said quietly, 'and I'm asking you if I scared you in bed. You weren't experienced, were you? And things grew pretty intense between us, pretty quickly. Was that part of the problem?'

Embarrassed by the images his words created, Millie looked down at the baby. 'We shouldn't be talking about this in front of him!'

'He's three months old,' Leandro said dryly. 'I don't feel the need to censor my conversation just yet. Answer my question. Did I scare you?'

'No.' What was it about him that made her body react like this? Her nipples were hard, pressing against her lace bra as if inviting his attention. 'You didn't scare me.'

'But you were shocked.'

Millie wished there was a drink nearby. Her mouth was suddenly as dry as the desert in a drought. 'I was a bit self-conscious.'

'Why?'

Because she hadn't been able to throw off the feeling that he must be comparing her to the beautiful women he usually dated. 'I don't know—you were just very bold and confident, I suppose. You didn't care if it was the middle of the day. And there was that time in your office—'

'Sex isn't restricted to the bedroom at night time.'

'I know—but in the dark I could have been anyone.'

'Which is why I like daylight.' Leandro let out a long breath, his exasperation obvious. 'This isn't good enough for me, Millie. You're saying that you'll think about it, but you obviously don't believe it's going to last. That doesn't work for me. I want your total commitment to making our marriage work.' His eyes were hard and she gave a sigh.

'All right, you told me to tell you when you were doing it and you're doing it now,' she croaked. 'You're being scary.'

He muttered something in Greek under his breath. 'Are

you sure "scary" isn't just a word you apply to a situation that isn't to your liking?'

'No. It's a word I apply to you. It's what you are when something doesn't meet with your approval. You're so used to getting your own way, you don't know how to compromise.'

Leandro looked startled. 'I am perfectly able to compromise.'

'What if you're the one who wants a divorce?'

'We weren't talking about divorce,' Leandro said silkily, 'we were talking about marriage.'

Millie stared down at the baby, finding the thought of marriage to Leandro quite impossibly daunting. Marriage meant bed and bed meant he'd find out…

How would he handle it? Would he turn away with revulsion? Or would he feel sorry for her and try and pretend he didn't care? Could men pretend? No, it was a physical thing— there would be no pretending.

'There will be no divorce,' he said firmly. 'Neither will there be any more turning your back on me. Or piling up resentment in your head and not telling me why you're glaring at me. This time, if something isn't working for you, I want to know why.' He was hard and uncompromising and she felt her heart lurch because she knew that he was going to be the one who stumbled this time.

And perhaps she wasn't being fair to him, not telling him the truth about what had happened since they'd last met.

But she just couldn't. Not yet.

He'd find out soon enough. And his reaction would decide the future of their marriage. And Costas's future.

Millie stared down at the baby, wishing she was young enough to have someone make her decisions for her. 'I'll think about it today.'

'I want my wife back, Millie. In every sense of the word.'
His gaze was hard and direct. 'No more headaches, no more
"too tired".'

'What if I *am* too tired?'

'I'll wake you up.' Leandro's eyes gleamed dark with
sexual intent. 'I was very patient and gentle with you last time
because I knew how inexperienced you were and I didn't
want to rush you. It was a mistake. A woman is never too tired
for good sex. There was something else going on and I should
have pushed you to tell me what it was.'

Millie's stomach cramped and the rush of heat in her pelvis
shocked her. 'What are you saying? That this time you're not
going to be patient or gentle?'

'That's right,' he said silkily, 'I'm not. This time we're going
to have an adult sexual relationship. I look forward to introduc-
ing you to the pleasures of truly uninhibited sex. In full daylight.'

Her face turned scarlet. 'You're trying to shock me.'

'No. But neither am I trying *not* to shock you, as I did
before.' His eyes lingered on her mouth. 'You're a very sexual
woman but we barely explored the surface the first time
round. This time, it's going to be different.'

'It might not be! Perhaps I won't find you attractive any
more!' The moment she said the words she realised how ridiculous they sounded and he obviously agreed because an
ironic smile played around his mouth.

'Do you want me to explore that statement further?'

'No.' Millie was grateful that she was holding the baby. 'I
don't. I don't want to talk about it at all.'

'Well, tough, because from now on no subject is off limits.'
His mobile phone buzzed insistently and Leandro retrieved
it from his pocket, registered the caller's name and then
looked at her face. 'What?'

'If I come back, I want you to switch off your phone when you're with us,' she said stiffly, 'otherwise Costas will grow up feeling second best to a mobile network.'

Leandro gave her a long look and then rejected the call with an exaggerated stab of his finger. 'Satisfied?'

Millie nodded, although she had no expectations that it would last. She really didn't need to worry about saying yes to coming back, Millie thought bleakly, because he'd be working all the time. He always did. She'd barely see him.

'I have one rule for our relationship,' he purred, dropping the phone back into his pocket. 'Just one.'

'Go on.'

'No matter what happens—you don't run off. You don't walk away from this marriage. You stay, no matter what.'

Millie licked her lips. 'What if you're the one who wants to run?'

'That isn't going to happen.'

'It might do.' She thought about everything that had happened to her and felt a lurch of unease. If things had been bad before, how much worse were they going to be this time around?

She was dreading the moment when he discovered the truth about what had happened to her.

Leandro wasn't a man to couch his true feelings under a soft blanket of political correctness or sensitivity, was he? He'd say what he thought.

And she knew what he was going to think.

And it would be like hammering nails into raw flesh.

Millie rocked the baby, afraid that her emotional turbulence might somehow communicate itself to the sleeping child and disturb him.

'I'll allow you the rest of the day to think it over.' Having delivered what he obviously considered to be a considerable compromise, Leandro strolled towards the door. 'I have a meeting in Paris. Feel free to fire the nanny and choose someone else. I will be back by tonight and you will give me the answer I want to hear. And after that I will be switching off my mobile phone. And if you feel even a flicker of a headache, I suggest you take a painkiller because I won't be allowing that as a valid excuse.'

CHAPTER FIVE

WHY had he allowed her time to think it over?

Surrounded by a room full of lawyers, Leandro drove the meeting at a furious pace, determined to close the deal that had been the main focus of his attention for six months. But he was aware that the timing was bad.

His mind on Millie, he was impatient to return to London.

He didn't trust her not to vanish, taking the child with her.

What evidence did he have that she was committed to their marriage? To the baby?

None.

On edge and impatient, he pushed through the agenda with supersonic speed, issuing orders, obtaining clarification on points he considered important, and ignoring issues that he considered irrelevant.

Having condensed what should have been an all-day meeting into a few intense hours, he rose to his feet and paced over to the window that ran from floor to ceiling along one side of the spectacular boardroom that dominated his Paris office. 'We're done here. Finish off. If you have any questions, you can speak to my team in London.'

The lawyer in charge of the deal picked up the thick pile

of papers that had formed the focus of the discussion. 'I wish everyone was as decisive as you. Clearly the abysmal state of the markets isn't keeping you awake at night.'

'No.' Something else was responsible for that. *His personal life.*

The man snapped his briefcase closed. 'I must congratulate you, Mr Demetrios. You have a quite startling ability to predict and understand human behaviour. Somehow you have still managed to make quite extraordinary profits even though the markets are collapsing around you. You anticipated the shift in the market before there were any outward signs. Stock in the Demetrios Corporation actually rose yesterday and yet market conditions have never been more challenging.'

'One person's challenge is another person's opportunity.' Distracted, Leandro kept his eyes fixed on the Paris skyline, his mind on his fragile marriage. *Was he mad, trying to save it?* Or was it like rare china dropped onto concrete? Shattered beyond repair.

In the past twenty-four hours he'd learned how little he knew about Millie.

Either that, or she'd changed. She was more…assertive. Or maybe she'd always been like that and he hadn't looked closely enough. Certainly there were plenty of aspects to her personality that he hadn't seen.

Leandro frowned. Had she really found him scary?

'Speculation about the parentage of the baby doesn't seem to have had an adverse effect on the price of your stock.' The voice of the lawyer broke into his thoughts and Leandro stilled.

'Our business is concluded for the day,' he said coldly. 'My assistant will show you out.'

Aware that he'd committed a gross error of judgement in

mentioning something so personal, the man turned scarlet and stammered an apology but Leandro didn't turn.

Perhaps he couldn't blame Millie for believing the worst of him, he thought grimly, *when the rest of the world was thinking it alongside her.*

His reputation had always been a matter of supreme indifference to him, but he was starting to realise that it was now coming back to bite him.

The lawyers rose, like a room full of children drilled in classroom etiquette, almost comical in their desperation to absent themselves.

Once the room was empty Leandro rolled his shoulders, trying to relieve the tension. He prowled the length of the boardroom, gazing through the floor-to-ceiling plate-glass window that allowed him to enjoy a view of the Seine as it snaked through the city.

A sense of foreboding came over him. He really shouldn't have left her.

He ran his hand over the back of his neck and withdrew his phone from his pocket. He'd speak to her—tell her that he'd be home in the next few hours. They'd spend some time together.

Tapping his foot, he waited for someone to answer.

And it was a long wait.

When the housekeeper finally answered the phone and informed him that both his wife and the baby had gone out, his tension levels increased tenfold. When he was told they'd gone out without a driver or a member of his security staff, Leandro abandoned thoughts of work for the rest of the day and ordered his car to be brought round to the front of the building.

She'd left.

She'd run again.

What had he expected?

'An astonishing ability to predict and understand human behaviour'—wasn't that what the lawyer had said?

Leandro gave a humourless laugh. Where had that ability been when it had come to understanding his own wife? If he'd studied her as closely as he studied the stock markets and company portfolios, he would never have left London.

At every turn, she surprised him. He hadn't expected her to show up at the house, he certainly hadn't expected her to offer to care for her sister's baby. And as for their relationship, he'd made a number of assumptions—assumptions he was now beginning to question. Her humble confession that she was 'ordinary' had revealed a depth of insecurity that he'd been unaware of. And the fact that he'd been unaware of it made him realise just how little he knew of her.

But he intended to rectify that.

If he wasn't already too late.

'Do you like this one? Shake it and it plays a tune, touch this bit and it's soft and furry, this bit is rough.' Millie held the toy over the pram. 'And you can chew the rings on the end. The book says you're going to want to start chewing fairly soon.'

Baby Costas gurgled quietly to himself and Millie leaned over and gently tucked the blanket more firmly around him. 'I suppose we'd better be getting back. I need the rest of the afternoon to get ready. Believe me, it takes me that long to look even vaguely presentable. And even then I won't look good enough for Leandro. If I'm going to tell him that I'll stay married to him, I need to look the part. Don't pull that face at me.' She smiled down at him. 'You try being married to someone who looks like him. It's hard work, trust me. Especially when you start off with a face and body like mine.

Come on—I'll just pay for these and then we'll wander home.'

She put the toy down on top of the pram. On impulse she added a little outfit that caught her eye. Then she made her way across the shop to pay. Standing in the queue, she stared down at Costas, automatically searching for a resemblance to Leandro.

'Oh, my—just take a look at that.' The girl in front of her in the queue gave a wistful sigh. 'What are the chances of my losing ten kilos in the next five seconds?'

'Forget it. Your best bet is to hope he likes curvy women,' her friend said gloomily, pulling in her rounded tummy.

'His type always go for the skinny sort.'

'With blonde hair.'

'*Straight,* long blonde hair.'

'He is truly spectacular. If I had him in my bed I might actually decide that sex was a more attractive option than sleep.'

'He's coming this way.'

'I'd give a million pounds just to be kissed by him once.'

Sensing the shift in the atmosphere and interested to know what kind of man could induce such enthusiasm among the members of her sex, Millie glanced up idly and saw Leandro striding purposefully across the store. Like a lion wandering into the middle of a herd of gazelle, the women all stared at him, transfixed.

Millie gave a whimper of horror. What was he doing here? Wasn't he supposed to be in Paris? She hadn't expected him to return to the house until dinnertime at the earliest. When they'd been together before, he'd frequently missed dinner, working late into the evening. But here he was, in the middle of the afternoon, clearly looking for her.

How had he known she was here?

Aware that any moment now he was going to spot her and

even more aware that she'd spent absolutely *no* time on herself since he'd last seen her, Millie slid out of the queue, turned her back and walked quickly towards the door.

The thought of him seeing her when she wasn't prepared filled her with horror. Even the 'natural' look took her hours to achieve.

Furtively she glanced over her shoulder, taking a round-about route via cots and prams so that he'd be less likely to notice her. She didn't want him to see her like this.

She'd planned to spend the rest of the afternoon getting ready to face him. *Ready to give him her answer.* True, her outward appearance wasn't going to make any difference at all to the eventual outcome of their relationship, but she knew she'd have more confidence with him if she was at least looking her best on the outside.

Another glance over her shoulder showed him frowning around the shop and Millie melted quietly out of the door, pondering on the fact that to be so ordinary as to be unnoticeable could be a blessing. In this instance, it had worked to her advantage, but once in a while it would be nice to be so beautiful that every man in the shop was staring at her.

Except that she didn't want every man in the shop, did she? She just wanted Leandro.

A hand closed over her shoulder. 'Excuse me, madam. I have reason to believe you're in possession of goods you haven't paid for.'

Millie froze. Several people passing turned to stare and she felt the hot singe of mortification darken her cheeks as she noticed the items she'd selected still sitting on top of the baby's pram. 'Oh, no.' She turned and looked at the uniformed security guard. 'I'm so sorry. I—I completely forgot that I'd picked them up.'

'Don't waste your time thinking up excuses.' The security guard's expression warned her that he was no soft touch. 'I've been watching you for a few minutes. You were behaving in an extremely suspicious manner. Instead of taking a direct route to the door, you took a roundabout route, ducking down and quite obviously trying not to be seen.'

'I *was* trying not to be seen,' Millie said quickly and saw his expression harden. 'I—I don't mean by you. I was…' Realising how much trouble she was in, she pressed her fingers to her forehead and the security guard's mouth tightened.

'We have a very strict policy about prosecuting shoplifters. I'd like you to come with me.'

'I'm not a shoplifter!' Her tone urgent, Millie put her hand on his arm, affronted that he'd think that of her. 'It was a genuine mistake.'

He withdrew his arm pointedly. 'If you just come back into the store, madam, you can explain it to the police.'

'No!' Millie was aware of the crowd gathering and wanted to disappear into a big hole in the ground. *Why was it,* she wondered desperately, *that people were so fascinated by other people's misfortunes?* What pleasure did they gain from standing around, staring? Not one of them had stepped in to support or defend her. She was on her own. 'You don't understand.' She licked her lips and tried one more time. 'This was an oversight, nothing more. I saw something—someone—'

'She saw me.' The deep masculine voice came from behind her and Millie suppressed a groan. She didn't need to look to know who it was. So much for not drawing attention to herself.

Great. Now her humiliation was complete. Not only was she looking a complete mess but she'd been behaving like a criminal.

'You know this lady?' The security guard squared his shoulders. 'She walked out without paying, sir.'

'And I'm afraid I take the blame for that.' Leandro's tone was a mixture of apology and smooth charm. 'She was up in the night with the baby. I'd given her strict instructions to rest today and not leave the house. Do you have children…' his gaze flickered to the man's identity badge '…Peter?'

'Two,' the man said stiffly. 'Boys.'

Leandro smiled his most charismatic smile. 'And I'm sure they've given you a few sleepless nights in their time.'

'You could say that.' Under Leandro's warm, encouraging gaze, the man relaxed slightly. 'There were days when the wife walked around in a coma. I remember she left the bath running one morning and flooded the entire house.'

'It's unbelievable that something as apparently small and innocent as a baby can cause so much disruption,' Leandro purred sympathetically. 'And unbelievable what sleep deprivation can do, Peter.' Having personalised the conversation, he put a hand on Millie's shoulder and kissed the top of her head. 'This is *all* my fault. Tonight, *agape mou*, I will take my turn with the baby and you will catch up on some sleep.'

There was a collective sigh among the crowd and the security guard looked undecided.

'I still have to take her back inside and call the police. That's my job.'

Millie opened her mouth to defend herself again but Leandro brought his mouth down on hers in a gentle but determined kiss that effectively silenced her. It only lasted seconds but when he lifted his head she was too flustered to do anything except gape at him.

He gave her a smile and pulled her into the protective circle of his arm, taking control of the situation. 'I understand that it isn't part of your job description to make individual judgements so I'm more than happy to be the one to present the details to the manager of the store and the police. I'm sure they'll understand. And perhaps we could talk to the local paper.' Leandro's voice was smooth as polished marble. 'It's ridiculous that you aren't allowed to exercise judgement on individual cases like this one. You should be allowed to take responsibility for your decisions.'

The man straightened his shoulders. 'In some circumstances I can make my own decisions, of course, it's just that—'

'You can?' Leandro looked impressed. 'Then it's lucky for us that *you* were the one on duty today. Someone as experienced as yourself will be able to tell the difference between a genuine mistake committed in a state of exhaustion and an attempt to steal.'

The security man flushed under the attention and then gave a nod. 'If you'll just take your purchases to the till, sir, I'll report to my superiors that this was all a genuine misunderstanding.'

'You're more than generous,' Leandro murmured, lifting the items from the top of the pram and glancing at Millie. 'This is all that you wanted, *agape mou?*'

Swamped with humiliation, still stunned that the brief kiss had affected her so much, Millie nodded mutely and stood there, clutching the pram for support while Leandro strode back inside the store with the security guard.

'Don't worry, love,' one of the women said to her, 'I was the same when my Kevin was born. Didn't get a wink of sleep for two years. I was so tired that I once found my car keys in the washing machine. At least you've got a gorgeous man willing to chip in. Mine didn't lift a finger for the first seven years of their lives. Now, if I'm lucky, he'll kick a football with them.'

Millie moved her lips to reply but she could still feel Leandro's mouth on hers, the latent sensuality in that brief kiss enough to have reawakened something she'd tried desperately hard to bury.

Nothing had changed, she thought helplessly. He still had the ability to turn her to a quivering wreck. Only this time things were a thousand times worse, her insecurities a thousand times deeper.

Leandro appeared by her side. He shot her a questioning look and then gave a knowing smile that indicated that he knew exactly why she was looking so dazed. Without comment, he handed her a bag and then guided her down the paved street towards the main road.

Desperate to escape from what felt like a hundred pairs of eyes, Millie stared straight ahead and then saw a burly man standing next to a sleek black Mercedes.

He sprang to attention as Leandro strode towards him and opened the rear door with military efficiency. 'If you take the baby, sir, I'll deal with the pram.'

Reluctant to be trapped with Leandro in a confined space, Millie stopped dead on the pavement but the firm pressure of Leandro's hand urged her towards the car. 'Inside, now,' he ordered, 'before you draw any more attention to yourself.'

'Does everyone always do exactly as you tell them?' Arching her back to free herself of his lingering touch, she stumbled into the warm cocoon of leather and luxury, shockingly aware of him. He slid in after her, holding the baby safely in the crook of his arm.

Only then did Millie notice the baby car seat.

With surprising gentleness, Leandro laid the baby in the car seat and strapped him in carefully. Then he sat down next to her, the length of his hard thigh brushing against hers.

The driver slid into the car, locked the doors and then pulled into the stream of traffic.

Millie shifted sideways in her seat. 'I wasn't expecting you back so soon.'

'Is that a complaint?'

'More of an observation. Since when did you work half-days?'

His eyebrow lifted in mockery. 'Since you made the rules.'

'I said it would be nice if you were home at some point before the middle of the night,' Millie muttered, stifled by how near he was, 'not halfway through the afternoon.'

'Is this going to be one of those conversations that a man can't possibly win?'

She flushed, realising that she sounded completely unreasonable. 'You shouldn't have kissed me in front of all those people. Why did you do that?'

'To stop you saying something that would have landed you in even more trouble. Every time you opened that mouth of yours, you dug a deeper hole in which to fall.' Leandro's gaze cool and assessing. '*What* did you think you were doing?'

'I—I wasn't thinking. I'm sorry I embarrassed you. I just forgot to pay.'

'I'm not talking about the shoplifting episode, I'm talking about the fact that you were walking around central London on your own.'

'I was shopping for the baby.'

'You left the house without telling anyone.'

'I didn't know I was *supposed* to tell anyone. You told me I could go shopping.'

His jaw tensed. 'I assumed you would have called your driver.'

Millie blinked. 'I have a driver?'

'Of course.'

'But I didn't want to go in the car. I wanted to walk,' she muttered. 'All the books say that babies like fresh air. And I needed the fresh air too. I wanted to think.'

'You didn't appear to be doing much thinking when you walked out of the shop without paying,' he said caustically, and she flushed.

'I walked out because I saw you. You flustered me.'

'I *flustered* you?' His eyes gleamed with sardonic humour. 'Exactly what made you "flustered"?'

'You did. Flustering everyone around you is what you do best.'

Leandro removed his tie and leaned back in his seat, a faint smile touching his mouth. 'I can see that I have a grossly inflated opinion of myself. So far, in our new spirit of honesty, I've discovered that I'm scary, intimidating and that I fluster you. I'm beginning to understand why you left. Who in their right mind would stay married to such an ogre?'

Remembering the circumstances of her departure, Millie glanced sideways at him only to find him watching her— *reading her with almost embarrassing ease.*

'Our problems started before that day,' he observed softly, and she didn't deny it.

'Our problems started the day I married you.'

'No. Our honeymoon was wonderful. The day we returned from our honeymoon. And I'm still trying to work out why.' A muscle flickered in his jaw. 'Did I change?'

'Yes.' Millie frowned. 'Or perhaps you didn't. Perhaps you were just being you. I just didn't know you that well. Once you were back in working mode, our relationship took a back seat to your business.'

'Just for the record, were there any parts of my behaviour that met with your approval?'

'I like the fact that you're confident.'

'Confidence is acceptable?'

She ignored the irony in his tone. 'As long as you're not so confident you make me feel like a waste of space.' Seeing one of his eyebrows lift, she gave an awkward shrug. 'When I can see you grinding your teeth and thinking, idiot, just because someone isn't as quick or as decisive as you, I *don't* like it.' Millie hesitated, naturally honest. 'But I can see why I annoyed you. I had no idea how to behave in your world.'

'You make it sound as if we are occupying parallel universes.' Leandro's lazy drawl was in direct contrast to his sharp, assessing gaze. 'I was under the impression that my world, as you call it, comes something close to female nirvana. You had access to unlimited funds and a lifestyle most people dream about.'

'Well, that's the thing about dreams, isn't it? They don't always turn out so well in reality. All the money in the world didn't save our marriage, did it?' Millie found it hard to think about that time. She turned to stare out of the window, trying not to think of how ecstatically happy she'd been. 'It wasn't real, was it? Those early days when we first met —it was like living in a bubble. We got married in a hurry without thinking through what we both wanted.'

'I knew what I wanted. I thought you did, too.'

'I suppose I didn't know what it was all going to involve.'

'Did it occur to you to talk to me about how you were feeling?'

'When?' Millie looked at him. 'You were always working. And when you weren't—well, you weren't that approachable. You were stern—'

'And intimidating—yes, I got that message.' Leandro seemed unusually tense. 'Just for the record, I had no idea you found me intimidating,' he said gruffly. 'Is that why you scurried out of the shop like a fugitive when you saw me arrive?'

'Partly. I wasn't expecting to see you.'

'You need notice?'

Millie touched her jeans self-consciously. 'I would have dressed up.'

His gaze slid down her body. 'You have fantastic legs. You look sexy in those jeans.'

Her heart danced. 'I—I thought you'd prefer me in a dress.' *And she didn't wear dresses any more.*

'You look sexy in everything. And nothing.' His velvety remark brought a blush to her cheeks and she felt slightly sick because she knew something that he didn't.

'What were you doing in the shop, anyway?'

'Looking for you.'

'Why not just wait for me in the house?'

Leandro drew in a breath. 'I had no reason to believe you'd be returning to the house.'

'You thought I'd run?'

'Yes.' He was characteristically direct. 'Do you blame me? It's what you did the last time. It's understandable that I'd be concerned that you won't do it again. Maybe it's time I introduced a little gentle bondage into our relationship,' he said softly. 'You were so innocent when I met you, I never did introduce you to the possibilities of velvet handcuffs. They might come in useful.'

A disturbingly erotic vision played across her brain and Millie felt the slow burn of awareness inside her. Everything she knew about sex, she'd learned from him. *And he was a master.* 'I'm not innocent any more. You took care of that.'

'We'd barely begun, *agape mou.*' Leandro relaxed in his seat, a dangerous smile playing around his mouth. 'But things will be different this time. This time we're going to talk.' He studied her, his dark eyes resting on her curling hair and then sliding to her faded jeans and her scuffed trainers. 'Today you look exactly the way you looked when I first met you.'

That bad?

Millie opened her mouth to apologise and then stopped herself. She'd spent a year trying to accept the way she was and she wasn't going to let him undo all that good work. She wasn't going to let being with him hammer holes in her confidence.

Self-conscious, she lifted a hand to her hair and then let it drop because she knew that it was going to take far more than a few tweaks of her fingers to turn her into a svelte groomed version of herself. She didn't need a mirror to know that her hair was curling wildly, falling past her shoulders in ecstatic disarray, as if relieved to have been given a break from her endless attempts to tame it.

It was a good job he worked so hard, she thought, biting back a hysterical laugh. It had taken her almost an entire day to tame her hair into the sleek, groomed look, apply her make-up, choose the right outfit.

'I'm dressed like this because I was shopping with the baby,' she said defensively. 'I wasn't expecting to see you.'

'It's lucky for you I found you…' Leandro stroked his fingers down the back of her neck '…or you'd currently be trying to talk your way out of shoplifting charges.'

'How *did* you find me?'

'My security team have inserted a tracking device into Costas's pram.'

'They *what?*' Millie looked at him in astonishment. 'Are you mad?'

'No, I'm security conscious. Which is more than you are.' Leandro's mouth tightened. '*Maledizione,* do you ever *think,* Millie? You are my wife. And you're walking around the streets pushing this baby in his pram. This baby with whom the whole world appears obsessed.'

'They're waiting for you to admit or deny that you're the father.' Her gaze settled on his but he held that gaze, as if challenging her to doubt him.

'Then they're going to be waiting a long time because I will never feel obliged to explain myself to strangers. I'm surprised you left the house with him. Why weren't you mobbed by journalists?'

'Because I sent the new nanny out earlier with a decoy pram.'

'A *decoy* pram?'

'Yes. After you left I rang the agency and they sent someone round straight away. I really liked her. We talked about the problem and decided that it wasn't fair for Costas to be housebound because of these people. So I suggested she leave the house with a doll in a pram. That's what she did. And she walked fast and kept her head down, like someone with something to hide. And they all followed her. Poor girl.' Still feeling guilty about that, Millie pulled a face. 'But I think she'll be all right. She's very down-to-earth.'

Leandro leaned his head back and laughed. 'I've *definitely* underestimated you. Nevertheless, it has to stop. There are people out there who would use you and the baby to get to me.'

Millie felt as though her stomach had been dropped off the side of a cliff. 'They'd kidnap the baby?'

'I don't want to frighten you. I receive threats occasionally—it comes with the territory,' he said carefully, 'and it's the job of my security team to work with the police to assess the risk. From now on I want you to take basic precautions.'

Instinctively, Millie put a hand on Costas's car seat and looked nervously out of the window.

'He will be fine.' Leandro leaned his head against the seat and closed his eyes, apparently undisturbed by the serious topic of the discussion. 'The car is bulletproof and my chauffeur is an expert in defensive driving.'

'*What?* You think someone's going to shoot at us? This gets worse and worse.' Millie was rigid on the edge of her seat, wondering how he could relax there with his eyes shut. 'And you think we live in the same world? Where I come from I don't need an armed guard to go to the supermarket.'

He didn't open his eyes. 'If going to the supermarket forms a high point in your day, I will arrange for them to open early for you. That way you can shop without a security hassle.'

Millie gave a choked laugh. 'You mean I can have first pick of the food.'

'If that's what you want. I would have thought scouring the shelves of the supermarket is an overrated pastime,' he murmured, 'but I've never claimed to understand women. From now on I want you to discuss your itinerary with Angelo and he will do whatever needs to be done to ensure your safety.'

'Who is Angelo?'

'The security guard that my team has selected for you. He's ex-special forces.'

'So he's going to abseil down the side of the house every morning in a black ski mask and bring me breakfast in bed?' Her caustic remark drew a wolfish smile from him and his eyes finally opened, like a predator who has discovered that there is something worth waking up for.

'No, *agape mou*. If he goes anywhere near your bedroom, he's fired. When you're naked between the sheets, I'll do the protecting.'

Trapped by the molten sexuality in his dark eyes, Millie felt her heart pound and her stomach tumble. Breathless, she dragged her eyes from his, only to find her gaze trapped by the hint of dark body hair visible at the base of his bronzed throat. Looking away from that had her noticing the width of his shoulders and in the end she just closed her eyes because the only way not to want him was not to look. And even then the delicious curl of awareness that warmed her belly didn't fade. *Help,* she thought desperately. Leandro possessed monumental sex appeal, and he knew it.

'Leandro.' Her voice was a croak of denial. 'It's been a year…'

'I know exactly how long it's been,' he purred softly, and Millie glanced at him and then immediately looked away, shaken by the look of sexual intent in his eyes.

'I don't know why you want me back,' she muttered, and he gave a soft laugh.

'You're my wife, Millie. And I expect my wife to stand by my side, no matter what.'

No matter what.

What was that supposed to mean? That she was supposed to overlook his affairs? *Was that what he was saying?*

Her stomach churned and the sick feeling rushed towards her, the same feeling she'd had when she'd seen him with her sister.

He was expecting her to spend a lifetime overlooking the fact that he had other women. Looking the other way while he took another woman to his bed. And she knew that every time she thought he was with someone else, a little piece of her would die.

Millie stared straight ahead, her expression blank.

What self-respecting woman would say yes to those terms?

CHAPTER SIX

'I'M JUST not like that. He might be my husband, but that doesn't give him the right to walk all over me. I'm not going to let him hurt me a second time.' Millie stuffed baby clothes into a holdall. 'That would make me stupid, wouldn't it?'

The baby cooed and kicked his legs.

'We're just *wrong* for each other. Why can't he see that? There's no point in me trying to talk to him about this because he's good with words and I'm not. With any luck he won't follow me. He didn't follow me the first time and I can't believe he wants a baby cramping his lifestyle.' Millie thought about the actress and then wished she hadn't. 'It isn't easy being married to a man every woman in the world wants. Unless you're the woman every man in the world wants. And I'm not.' Dwelling on that dismal thought, she closed the bag.

'"*I expect my wife to stand by my side no matter what.*" Obviously I'm expected to watch while he smiles at models and actresses.' She stowed the bag under the cot out of sight. 'Well, I can't do that. I've spent a year trying to get over him. I'm not putting myself through that again.'

'What are you not putting yourself through again?' Leandro stood in the doorway and Millie jumped.

'B-being chased by j-journalists,' she stammered. Her heart thumping, smothered with guilt, she scooped Costas up in her arms and then faced Leandro.

He was dressed in black jeans and a casual shirt and he looked every bit as sexy as he did in a suit.

No wonder she hadn't been able to hold him, she thought miserably. He was stunning.

She'd be doing him a favour by leaving.

He didn't want her and he didn't want a baby.

He wanted a life.

Clearly undisturbed by her emotional turbulence, Costas fell asleep on her shoulder and Leandro gave a faint smile.

'Someone is tired. Put him to bed and come and eat. We need to make plans.'

It obviously hadn't occurred to him that she might refuse.

Faced with no alternative, Millie followed him to the dining room, but she was too nervous to eat and too nervous to talk. Pushing the food around her plate, her mind explored the safest route and means of transport.

Leandro lounged across from her, relaxed and watchful, as if he was trying to get inside her head.

Millie was frantically searching for reasons not to share his bed when a member of staff approached him and delivered a message.

His mouth tightening, Leandro stood up and dropped his napkin on the table. 'I apologise. This is one call I have to take. After this there will be no more, I promise.'

'Don't worry about it. I'll go and check on Costas.' Almost weak with relief, Millie seized on the excuse to go and hide away with the baby. Maybe she should leave now, except that it was too late in the day and the trains would soon stop running.

No, it had to be tomorrow. But early.

Exhausted after the events of the past few days, she lay down on the bed in Costas's room and immediately fell asleep.

Leandro opened the door of the baby's room, his mouth tightening as he saw Millie asleep on the bed. Her hair was loose and tangled, her cheeks prettily flushed and her body curled up, very much like the baby who slept in the cot next to her.

She was avoiding sex again, he thought grimly. The obvious reason was that she hadn't forgiven him for his 'affair' with her sister, but Leandro knew that their problems went much deeper than that. She'd been avoiding sex long before the 'pool incident' as he now called it.

But whatever the reason, in the end she'd walked out. To him, that was an unpardonable sin that nothing could excuse.

Cold fingers of the past slid over his shoulder and he shrugged them away, refusing to dwell anywhere other than the present. That was what he did, wasn't it? He moved forwards. Always, he moved forwards.

Was that why he was so angry with Millie? *Because her actions had forced him to remember a time that he'd tried to forget?*

His disappointment in her was as fresh today as it had been a year ago.

Disappointment in her, or himself?

Was it his pride that was damaged? Because he'd got her wrong? He'd seen something in her that hadn't been there. On the day of their wedding she'd told him how much she wanted babies and he'd congratulated himself on finding the perfect wife and mother.

He'd thought she was a woman who would stand and fight. Instead, she'd walked out at the first opportunity.

Acknowledging that failure in his judgement hadn't grown any easier over the past year, Leandro mused as he left the nursery and walked towards his own suite of rooms.

So why had he insisted that she stay? Was he a masochist?

No. But his expectations of his wife had been seriously modified.

He'd give the child a home, he'd promised himself that he'd do that.

And as for his wife—well, he'd long ago learned how to lust without love, so that shouldn't be a problem.

Swearing in Greek, he yanked his shirt off and strode into the bathroom. Given that Millie had chosen to sleep with the baby, a cold shower was the only solution.

'Life won't be as fancy with me,' Millie told Costas as she strapped him in the car seat inside the taxi. 'None of this mood-altering lighting system, comfort cooling and under-floor heating. If your feet are cold, you wear socks, OK? It's a simple life, but I *can* promise I won't ever leave you. I know I left him, but that was different. I'll explain it to you when you're older.' It was still dark outside and she'd slipped out through the garden, careful to avoid any journalists who might still be camped at the front of the house. 'I've been renting a little flat in a village near the coast. I think you'll like it.'

She saw the taxi driver glance in his mirror and coloured. He probably thought she was mad, talking to a baby.

Or maybe he'd recognised her.

That horrifying possibility had had her sliding down in her seat, but then she told herself that she was being paranoid.

Who was going to look twice at her?

She'd pushed the pram and carried her bag and the car seat

to the next street so that no one would see her emerging from Leandro's house and make the connection.

The driver pulled up outside the train station. He helped her with the pram and the car seat and Millie gave him a generous tip, trying not to think what that money would have bought her.

'There's another half an hour until our train leaves, so we'll find a coffee shop and see if they'll warm your bottle.'

Even this early in the morning, the station was busy, and Millie weaved her way through suited men and women, all of whom appeared to be in a hurry.

She found a quiet corner in a coffee shop, bought herself a cappuccino and lifted Costas out of his pram to give him his bottle.

She was so engrossed in the business of feeding him that she didn't notice anyone else in the coffee shop until a light almost blinded her.

With a murmur of shock, Millie glanced up and what felt like a million cameras flashed.

Horrified, Millie snatched Costas's blanket and threw it around him, concealing him from the cameras. 'Go away!' She recoiled from the intrusive lenses, all pointed in her direction. 'What are you doing here?'

'The whole world wants to know about the Demetrios baby.'

'Well, the whole world should just mind its own business,' Millie snapped, her eyes searching for an escape route. There was none. The row of journalists between her and the door was now three deep and she could see other people in the station glancing across in curiosity, wondering what was happening.

How could she not have noticed?

Because she hadn't been looking for it. She wasn't used to living her life looking over her shoulder.

'Are you happy to look after the kid? Can't be easy for you.' The rough male voice came from right next to her and Millie turned her head and saw a man in shabby clothes sitting at the table next to her, a tape recorder in his hand.

Had he been there when she'd arrived? No, he'd arrived soon afterwards—which meant he must have followed her.

Hands shaking, Millie started to put Costas back in the pram but the photographers pressed closer, determined to get a shot of his face.

As one particularly persistent journalist stretched out a hand to move the blanket, Millie shifted Costas safely to one side. Her protective instincts going into overdrive, she gave her coffee a small nudge.

The hot liquid spilled over his arm and he cursed fluently, hopping backwards and glaring at her.

'Don't you dare use bad language in front of my child,' Millie snarled, but she was shaking so badly she could hardly speak. And she had no idea what to do. The crowd was building by the minute and she was trapped.

Seeing the determination in their eyes, she did the only thing she could do.

Still holding Costas protectively, she dragged her phone out of her pocket and called Leandro.

She'd expected him to be furiously angry with her for leaving, but instead their interchange was brief and to the point as he demanded to know her exact location and then ordered her to stay where she was and not move.

Looking at the pack of journalists pressing in on her, Millie gave a strangled laugh. Move? How?

Leandro arrived shortly after, the fact that he was unshaven simply adding to the aura of menace that shimmered around his muscular frame as he strode into the small coffee shop.

Radiating power and authority, Leandro said something to the journalists that she didn't catch, but it clearly had an effect because they fell back and a few of them melted away into the station. Millie thought she even heard one of them mutter an apology, but she couldn't be sure.

Wishing she had a morsel of Leandro's presence, she stood up shakily and lowered Costas into the pram, still shielding him from the cameras with her body.

'Is this all you brought?' Leandro picked up her bag, his handsome face taut and unsmiling as he gathered her things.

'Bag, pram, car seat,' Millie muttered, wondering whether she should have just taken her chances with the journalists. 'I'm *not* coming home with you.'

'We're not discussing this here.' He scooped up the car seat in his other hand and stood aside to let her pass. 'Let's move, before we attract any more attention.'

'Is it possible to attract any more attention than this?'

Her remark drew a faint smile from him. 'Believe it or not, yes.'

'I didn't think they had much of a story,' she murmured, and Leandro looked at her with naked exasperation.

'You just gave them a story, Millie. Don't you know *anything* about the media?'

'No. Just as I don't know anything else about your life. Now do you see why our marriage won't work?' Angry with herself for doing something so stupid, humiliated and close to despair, she stalked towards the entrance. Only then did she see the four bulky men from Leandro's security team positioned there.

Wondering why he'd tackled the journalists himself instead of using the heavyweights he'd brought with him, Millie walked through them with as much dignity as she could muster. Which wasn't much.

For a woman who didn't want any attention, she wasn't doing very well, she thought miserably, her face flaming with embarrassment as, protected by a circle of male testosterone, she moved through the now crowded station.

People stopped walking and stared and she could almost hear them wondering why a woman who looked like her required an entourage to keep her safe.

As she walked through the front of the station she would have paused but Leandro's palm was in her back, urging her towards the sleek dark car parked in the no parking zone.

As she slipped inside, the doors locked and the driver pulled away, the security team following in a different vehicle.

Millie braced herself for confrontation, but Leandro said nothing. Instead he drew his phone out of his pocket and made a single call, speaking in rapid Greek.

Moments later the car sped through the gates of his drive, through the private courtyard and straight into the garage. From there they were able to walk into the house without being seen while Leandro's driver used the car lift to take the car down to the basement garage.

Millie stood in the stunning double-height entrance atrium, lit by the skylight far above. She felt small and insignificant and wondered how Costas could possibly still be asleep after so much drama.

Leandro put her bag down in the hallway, left his staff to deal with the pram and gave instructions for the nanny to take charge of the baby. Then he propelled Millie into the beautiful conservatory that wrapped itself around the back of his enormous house.

The room was full of exotic plants, but Millie was too despondent to derive any comfort from the beauty of her surroundings.

'You left again.' His tone was raw and she flinched, wondering why he even cared.

'I didn't leave the baby,' she muttered. 'I left *you*. You want me to overlook the fact that you're going to have affairs, but I won't do that, Leandro. I won't grow old and grey watching while you play around with other women. Maybe that's what other Greek wives do, but I couldn't live like that.'

'Play around with other women? When did I say I wanted to play around with other women?' He looked stunned by the suggestion and she lifted her chin defensively.

'You said I was supposed to stand by your side, no matter what,' she reminded him. 'I assume "no matter what" means "no matter who I go to bed with". I can't turn a blind eye. It's asking too much.'

'"No matter what" means you and I standing together, facing whatever life throws at us.' His tone rang with incredulity. 'I said nothing about affairs. I have no intention of having affairs. I want you in my bed. No one else.'

Her assumptions having exploded into the atmosphere, Millie stood uncertainly, knowing that he'd change his mind once she was undressed. 'What if you discover the chemistry isn't there any more?'

Leandro moved so quickly she didn't see it coming. One moment he was facing her, legs apart in a confrontational stance; the next he was right in front of her, his hand on the back of her neck and his mouth on hers. And he knew exactly how to kiss to ensure maximum response. With the erotic exploration of his mouth and tongue, Leandro turned a kiss into something indescribably good and as Millie felt her grip on reality sliding away, her last coherent thought was that if she died now, she'd die happy.

Only after several minutes during which she lost track of

time and place did he finally lift his head. 'I don't foresee a problem.' He stepped back with all the easy confidence of a man who has proved his point and Millie ran shaking hands over her jeans, not sure whether to slap him or slide her arms round his neck and beg him to kiss her again.

'You shouldn't have done that.'

'People have been saying that to me all my life. If I'd listened to them, I'd still be playing in the dust on a remote Greek island.' Maddeningly relaxed, he glanced at his watch. 'Make up your mind, Millie. I'm only going to ask this *once*. Are you staying or going?'

Knowing that he'd dump her soon enough when he found out what had happened to her, Millie nodded. 'Staying.' At least then she could spend time with Costas.

'Good. I'll instruct my people to put out a statement saying that we are adopting the baby. Hopefully that will kill the story.'

'If I come back to you, I'll be surrounded by media.'

'As my wife you'll have more protection than if you go it alone. This morning has proved that.'

'But Costas and I can't leave the house without a bodyguard and a driver! What sort of life is that?'

'A privileged one,' Leandro drawled, ignoring the buzz of his phone. 'But while they're hovering like hyenas, we'll stay elsewhere.'

'We're leaving London?'

'This media circus presents a risk to the baby. I don't want to have to go through the courts to keep his picture out of the papers.'

Millie bit her lip. 'Where are we going?' It was touching that he was so protective, but at the same time it was upsetting because she could only see one reason why he would care so much for the baby's welfare.

'We're flying to Spiraxos later this morning. I just have some important calls to make.'

'We're going to Greece?' Her heart dropped. He'd taken her to his island on their honeymoon and they'd had three weeks of sun, sea and sex. Three indulgent weeks during which she'd been so happy. At that point in their relationship none of their problems had surfaced. She'd been ecstatically happy and so wildly in love that she'd woken up every morning with a smile on her face. The thought of returning there now made her feel sick. It would be like a cruel taunt, reminding her of that magical time before her life had fallen apart. 'Why Greece?'

'Because the island will give us privacy. And because our relationship was perfect when we were in Greece.' His gaze was bold and direct. 'We had an incredible time there. And if we're going to put the pieces of our marriage together, I'd rather the details of our reconciliation weren't documented in the pages of sleazy celebrity magazines. We will be able to relax, away from the eyes of the world.'

Relax? How could she possibly relax, trapped with him on Spiraxos, where she'd once spent the happiest time of her life? How could she relax, knowing what was coming? 'I—I'm not ready to fly to Greece. I need some time.'

'My staff will make any necessary preparations. All you have to do is walk onto my plane. And if you're worried about clothes, I can tell you now that you're not going to need any. Last night you slept alone, but tonight, *agape mou*...' Leandro flashed her a dangerous smile '...well, let's just say you won't be dressing for dinner.'

Tonight?

It was tonight.

No more excuses.

Millie's stomach churned horribly.

He was going to fly her all that way, only to discover that he didn't want to be with her any more.

It was going to be the shortest reconciliation on record.

Millie checked Costas again, grateful for any excuse to delay joining Leandro on the sun-baked terrace that overlooked the sparkling blue Aegean sea.

The journey to Greece had been smooth. Costas had slept most of the way and Leandro had spent his time reading and deleting endless emails, which meant she'd had far too much time to brood on the evening ahead of her.

Now that it had arrived, she couldn't bring herself to walk down to the terrace.

She was dreading the inevitable rejection.

'Are you planning to eat dinner with the baby? You have a hidden passion for baby milk perhaps?' Leandro's smooth, masculine tones came from behind her and she jumped because she hadn't expected him to come looking for her.

'I was just making sure he's all right.'

'Of course he's all right. He slept for the entire journey and now he's asleep again, which means, *agape mou*, that you have no excuse for not joining me.'

'Why?' Millie heard the ring of desperation in her own voice. 'Why would you want my company?'

'Because that's what married couples do. They eat dinner together.'

'Perhaps I'd better stay with the baby, just for tonight,' she hedged, 'in case he's unsettled after the journey.'

'He's asleep.'

'He might wake up and realise he's in a new environment.'

'In which case he'll yell. One of Costas's qualities is that he isn't shy about letting you know he's unhappy,' Leandro said dryly, staring down at the baby with a faint smile on his handsome face. 'All the bedrooms open onto the terrace, you know that. If he cries, we'll hear him.'

'I don't like leaving him.'

'We have a team of eight staff here, including the nanny that you appointed yourself.'

'He doesn't know them yet!'

'Neither is he likely to, if you don't allow them near him. Enough, Millie. The baby is going to be asleep!' His tone held a note of exasperation. 'Why is it that you're afraid to spend an evening with me? I've made a particular effort to be approachable and thoughtful. Am I such an ogre?'

She shook her head. 'No.'

Leandro gave an impatient sigh and slid his fingers under her chin. 'I am *trying* to understand what is going on here,' he breathed, 'and you're not giving me any clues. I thought you loved Spiraxos. I thought you'd be pleased to be here.'

'It's very quiet.' She meant that she found the intimacy difficult, but he misinterpreted her words.

'I'll arrange a few shopping trips it that's what's bothering you.'

Preoccupied by what was to come, Millie barely heard him. 'Why would that help? I'm not interested in shopping.'

'Millie.' His tone was dry. 'You used to spend hours deciding what to wear, so don't tell me you're not interested in clothes. I've never known a woman spend so long staring into her wardrobe.'

Because she'd had no idea what to wear. She'd been desperately insecure and those insecurities had grown and grown, fed by his gradual withdrawal. The harder she'd tried, the more he'd backed off until it had become obvious to her that he'd deeply regretted the romantic impulse that had driven him to marry her. And how much more insecure was she now? If she'd found it hard being his wife a year ago, now it seemed a thousand times harder.

This was the perfect opportunity to tell him everything that had happened to her after she'd walked out that day, but Millie just couldn't get the words past her lips.

'Given that you're so dedicated to the baby's welfare,' Leandro drawled, 'I will watch him while you take a shower and change for dinner. Remembering how long it used to take you, I'll prepare myself for a long wait.'

Millie cast a last reluctant look into the cot, willing Costas to wake up and yell. *Willing him to give her an excuse to miss dinner.* But for once he lay quietly, sleeping with a contented smile on his tiny mouth, oblivious to her silent signals and growing distress.

Which meant that she'd run out of excuses.

Leandro glanced at his watch and sprawled in the nearest chair with a sigh of resignation. Previous experience told him that he was going to be in for a serious wait. The length of time Millie took to get ready had been one of the things that had driven him crazy about her.

Not at first, of course. When they'd first met he'd been startled and charmed by how unselfconscious and natural she was. She couldn't bear to be away from him, even for a moment. Any time spent in the bathroom had been together. Making love. Touching.

She'd been addicted to him, and so affectionate that it had astonished him. Accustomed to women who guarded their behaviour and protected themselves, he'd never met anyone as free and honest with their emotions as Millie. She'd been as straightforward and honest as the fruit that grew on her parents' farm.

Or so he'd thought.

It had all changed on the day they'd arrived in London after their honeymoon.

Suddenly she'd morphed into one of those women he'd spent his adult life mixing with. She'd become obsessed with her appearance. It was as if she'd become a different person. Leandro had given up surprising her at home for a few stolen hours of daytime passion because she'd never been there. She'd spent her days in beauty salons and her nights out partying with him. And she'd spent hours scouring the celebrity gossip, looking for pictures of herself.

Leandro, up to his ears in work as usual, had been unable to work out what had happened to the girl he'd married. Had it all been an act designed to trap him and then she'd shown her true self? Or had it been marriage to a billionaire that had changed her? After all, up until her marriage with him she hadn't had the funds to allow her to indulge her apparent obsession with clothes and beauty products.

And yet over the past two days she'd seemed almost oblivious to her appearance.

Whoever said that women were a mystery hadn't been exaggerating, Leandro mused, stretching out his legs and making himself comfortable.

He looked at the sleeping baby and felt a rush of emotion that shook his self-control.

Alone, abandoned, a mother who had used him as a pawn…

Determined not to continue down that path of thought, he dug his BlackBerry out of his pocket, intending to distract himself with work. Then he heard a noise and glanced up to find Millie standing in the door of the dressing room, which connected directly to both bathroom and bedroom.

Leandro slipped his phone back into his pocket. 'That was quick.' He scanned her appearance, noticing with surprise that she'd left her hair curling and loose in its natural state and that the only make-up she was wearing was a shimmer of clear gloss on the curve of her lips. She was wearing a simple green top over a pair of trousers. 'I was expecting to wait at least an hour while you picked your outfit.'

Colour touched her cheeks and she gave a wan smile. 'There didn't seem much point in that. I'm no longer trying to impress you.'

Leandro frowned. 'Is that what you used to do?'

'Obviously I wanted to look my best.' She stooped, sliding her slender feet into the pair of shoes she was carrying.

Still pondering on her comment, he noticed that the only concession to her old look was a pair of killer heels. 'You never used to wear trousers.'

There was something in her expression that he couldn't read. 'I find trousers comfortable. Is it a problem?'

'Not at all.' They had problems far deeper than her choice of wardrobe, he mused, watching as she walked across to the cot and checked the baby again. Something was very wrong with her, and he had no idea what. 'Are you ready? Alyssa has laid dinner on the terrace.'

Millie stared down at the baby as if willing him to wake up and save her, and Leandro stared at her frozen profile in mounting frustration, searching for clues.

Was she looking at the baby, wondering if it was his? Or was there something more going on here?

Reaching into the cot, she tucked the sheet tenderly

around the sleeping baby and then withdrew her hand slowly. 'I'm ready.'

She spoke the words like someone preparing to walk to their doom and her whole demeanour was such a dramatic contrast from the last time they'd stood in this villa that Leandro wanted to close his hands around her shoulders and demand answers.

But his years in business had taught him when to speak and when to stay silent and he chose to stay silent, his expression neutral as he urged her towards the terrace.

The evening was only just beginning, he reminded himself. *They had plenty of time.*

CHAPTER SEVEN

MILLIE felt sicker and sicker. Wishing the baby would wake up and rescue her, she pushed the food from one side of her plate to the other, unable to face the thought of challenging her churning stomach by eating.

Candles flickered on the centre of the table and the silence of the warm evening was disturbed only by the insistent chirping of the cicadas and the occasional splash as birds skimmed the beautiful infinity pool, stealing water.

Across from her, Leandro said nothing. He lounged with masculine grace, his relaxed stance in direct contrast to her own mounting agitation. He wore a casual polo shirt, the simplicity of his clothing somehow accentuating his raw masculinity. *Whatever he wore, he looked spectacular,* she thought helplessly, putting her fork down and giving up the pretence of eating. The beauty was in the man himself, not in the way he presented himself. It didn't matter whether his powerful shoulders were showcased by an elegantly cut dinner jacket or a piece of simple cotton fabric, Leandro was all man. And that fact simply increased the churning in her stomach.

Or perhaps it was just because she was now more conscious than ever of the differences between her and the women he usually mixed with.

Had he had an affair?

The question played on her mind over and over again, a relentless torment fed by her own massive insecurities.

It was typical that he didn't try and put her at her ease, she thought desperately. He was so confident himself, he never thought that someone else might not be so comfortable in a situation.

'Alyssa must have been slaving all day,' she said, making polite conversation. 'The food is fantastic.'

'Then why aren't you eating any of it?'

'I'm not that hungry.'

Leandro leaned across and spooned some creamy *tzatsiki* onto her plate. 'When I first met you, you were always hungry. When I took you out to dinner, you ate three courses.'

'I had a very physical job,' Millie said defensively. 'I worked on a farm. If I didn't eat properly, I would have passed out.'

Leandro sat back in his chair, watching her across the table. 'Now I've upset you and I have no idea why.'

'You were criticising me.'

He tilted his head and she could see him rerunning the conversation through his brain. 'Exactly how and when did I criticise you?'

'You complained that I ate three courses, and—'

'It wasn't a complaint. It was a comment.'

'Same thing.'

'No, Millie,' he said gently, an ironic gleam in his eyes. 'It is *not* the same thing.'

'You mix with women who don't eat.' She ignored the food he'd put on her plate. 'In the circles you move in, eating is a bigger sin than adultery or wearing the wrong shade of pink.

All the women are thin. A visible rib cage is as much a status symbol as a pair of Jimmy Choos. So when you point out I ate three courses, what am I supposed to think?'

His gaze was thoughtful. 'You could think that the fact that you enjoy food and eating is one of the things I like about you.'

'Actually, I couldn't,' Millie said hotly, the defensive movement of her head sending her hair spilling around her face. 'Because I'm seeing no evidence to back it up. Apart from your momentary lapse with me, all the women you mix with clearly share DNA with stick insects. Take that actress— she's enough to give any normal woman a complex and a major eating disorder.'

He inhaled slowly. 'Your weight is clearly an issue.'

Millie played with her fork. 'You noticed that? I'm a woman,' she said sweetly. 'Of course my weight is an issue.'

'You have a fabulous body.'

'By fabulous, you mean fat.'

'I mean fabulous.' His eyes gleamed with lazy amusement and a trace of exasperation. 'Clearly I need a man-woman dictionary. Man says "fabulous", woman translates that into meaning "fat". Are there any other words in this unfathomable language I'm likely to need help with?'

'I'll let you know as we go along.'

'Thank you.' His tone dry, he leaned forward, and spooned some spicy sausage onto her plate next to the *tzatsiki*. 'Eat. Alyssa has spent all day in the kitchen in honour of your arrival. She remembered that you loved all Greek food, especially this. It was your favourite.'

'That was until someone told me how many calories were in each spoonful.'

'*Who* told you?'

'Oh, someone.' Millie felt the colour flood into her cheeks as she recalled that particular encounter. 'I expect she thought she was doing me a favour. Helping me fit into the strange world you live in.'

'I live in the same world as you, Millie.'

She glanced around her, looking at their privileged surroundings. 'If you think that, you're deluded. You move in a whole different world to most people, Leandro. It's no wonder I didn't fit.'

He was very still. 'Is that what you think?' His tone was soft. 'That you didn't fit?'

'It doesn't take a genius to see I wouldn't have had too much in common with some those waif-like celebrities you called your friends. My idea of a facial was splashing cold water to wake myself up at five in the morning during the harvest.'

He didn't answer immediately but she sensed a new tension about him and bit her lip, feeling suddenly guilty.

'Sorry,' she muttered. 'I didn't mean to criticise your friends. I'm sure they're lovely people. It wasn't their fault. If you drop a baby elephant into the middle of a flock of elegant swans, you've got to expect to startle them.'

Leandro's eyes glittered dark in the candlelight. 'And are you supposed to be the baby elephant in that analogy?' He sounded stunned. 'That's how you felt?'

Unsettled by his prolonged scrutiny, Millie shifted in her chair. 'How did you think I felt?'

A muscle flickered in his jaw and he toyed with the stem of his elegant wineglass. 'Honestly? I didn't think about it. Unlike you, I don't look for hidden meanings. Clearly I should have done.'

'Not all communication is verbal, Leandro.'

'Evidently not. But given your talent for reading me incorrectly, I think we'd better stick to the verbal sort for the time being. Tell me why you're not eating tonight.'

'My stomach is churning. I feel...sick.'

His dark brows met in a concerned frown. 'You're ill?'

'No. Just nervous.'

'Of what?'

'You, of course.'

His eyes held hers. 'I make you feel sick?' The incredulity in his tone made her wish she'd kept her mouth shut.

'Just a little bit.' Her cheeks turned pink. 'Well, quite a lot, actually.'

Leandro put the glass down on the table. 'Why?'

'I don't know. I'm not a psychologist. Maybe I'm seriously screwed up about you. But I think it's probably just the effect you have on me. Billionaire marries farm girl. It's pretty obvious that farm girl is going to have some major insecurities.'

'Billionaire marries farm girl,' he countered, 'and her insecurities vanish.'

'They double.'

'The way you think is a mystery to me.'

'Obviously.'

He rose to his feet and dropped his napkin onto the table. His mouth was set and determined, his eyes never once leaving her face as he stood next to her. 'Come.'

Millie looked at his outstretched hand. 'Why? Where are we going?'

'To put your insecurities to rest once and for all,' he purred, drawing her to her feet in a firm, decisive movement that brought her into contact with his hard, athletic frame. 'I intend to closely examine every curve of your fabulous body—and I mean fabulous, *not* fat,' he breathed, covering her lips with his fingers so that she couldn't interrupt, 'and by the time I've finished with you, your insecurities will be in a puddle on the floor along with your clothes.'

But that wasn't what was going to happen, was it? Millie's heart pounded. She thought of her body. *Thought of what he didn't know.* 'I really wanted an early night.'

'For once we agree on something.' His eyes gleamed with sexual promise. 'An early night followed by a lie-in. And another early night. The two might actually run together.'

Millie swallowed, her nerves almost snapping as she thought about the inevitable fallout of him taking her to bed. 'I can't— I just can't— I need some time.'

'I gave you time, Millie.' His voice was steady. 'I gave you space. And it was a mistake. All it did was widen the gulf between us. This time around we're doing things a different way. My way.'

'So I don't have a choice.'

His eyes shimmered with amusement. 'No, *agape mou,*' he murmured. 'There is no need to take on that martyred expression. I'm going to get to know you. Inside and out. In the past two days you have revealed more about yourself than you did in the entire time we were together. I am starting to realise that I didn't know you at all, but that is going to change from this moment onwards.' He trailed a finger over her flushed cheek. 'From now on I want to know everything in your head. And I won't let you shut me out.'

Standing in the bathroom, Millie pulled the robe tightly around her.

What was the best way to play this? Did she undress and walk into the bedroom naked? Or did she let him undress her?

Either way, it was going to be a disaster.

This was the moment she'd been dreading.

What was the point in putting it off any longer? Better to get it over with because the anticipation of what was to come was making her sick.

How would he react?

Forcing herself to move, she pushed open the door and stood for a moment, looking at him.

Leandro was sprawled on his back on the bed, eyes shut. His chest was bare and the light by the bed sent golden shadows across his sleek, bronzed shoulders.

In the year they'd been apart, he hadn't changed. Millie's gaze rested on the tangle of dark hair across the centre of his chest and then moved lower. He was naked, but he'd always been comfortable with his body, hadn't he? And no wonder. He was astonishingly fit, his physique strong and masculine.

His astonishing good looks had attracted the attention of the most beautiful women in the world.

Why did he want her? Was it just that he didn't believe in divorce? Was that the fragile bond that held them together?

Unable to see another possibility, she lost her confidence and would have slid back into the bathroom if his voice hadn't stopped her.

'If you run again, I'll come after you. And if you lock the door, I'll break it down. Your choice.'

Millie froze, her heart pounding frantically against her chest. But she moved forward, her legs stiff, as if they were trying to plead with her to take a different course of action. 'It isn't a choice, is it? You're not giving me a choice.'

'You made your choice when you decided to come back to me.' His eyes were open now, and he was watching her with that shimmering masculine gaze that always turned her stomach upside down. 'Come into the light where I can see you.'

Millie gripped the clasp of her robe tightly, wondering

whether she was actually going to have the courage to go through with this.

She stood there shivering and he frowned and sprang from the bed, prowling across to her with surprising grace for such a powerfully built man.

Leandro closed his fingers over her shoulders and forced her to look at him. 'I want to know what you're thinking.'

'Trust me, you don't.' Millie shook her head, the tears sitting in her throat like a brimming cup just waiting to overflow. She couldn't cry now. Later. *There'd be plenty of time for that later.*

With a growl of frustration, he scooped her face into his hands and lowered his head to kiss her. 'I don't understand why you are so insecure. You are a very beautiful woman.'

Her courage failed.

Maybe, just maybe, if he hadn't said those exact words she would have gone through with it.

'I'm not beautiful,' she croaked, dragging herself out of his arms. 'I'm *not* beautiful. And I can't do this. I just can't.'

'Why? Is this about what you think happened with your sister?'

'No, no, it isn't. It's about what happened to *me*. It's hopeless. I'm sorry, Leandro. I'm sorry.' Before he could stop her, Millie stumbled out of the room. Blinded by tears, she banged against the doorframe in her haste to get away from him, but the sudden pain in her arm was eclipsed by the far greater pain in her heart. She took refuge in one of the guest suites at the far end of the villa. Stumbling into the bathroom, she locked the door securely behind her and slid to the floor without bothering to switch on the lights.

It was impossible. The whole situation was impossible.

She should never have allowed him to blackmail her into

giving their marriage another try. She just should have stood there, told him what had happened and walked out while she still had some shred of dignity left. And she should have found another way of being close to her nephew. Visits. Letters. Photos. Anything other than this.

Why had she agreed to stay?

Had some small, stupid part of her hoped that this horrible situation could still have a happy ending?

In the pit of despair, she let the tears fall.

The door crashed open and she gave a jerk of shock.

Leandro stood there, a powerful figure silhouetted against the light of the bedroom. 'Every time you lock a door between us I'll break it down,' he vowed thickly, 'and every time you run I *will* find you.' With a soft curse, he flipped on the light and then sucked in a breath as it illuminated her ravaged features. His eyes fixed on her blotched, tear-stained face and his jaw tightened.

'Millie? What the *hell* is going on?' His voice was hoarse and he spread his hands in a gesture of helplessness. 'Why are you crying? *Maledizione,* I *never* wanted to upset you like this. Stop it, *agape mou.* Nothing is this bad.'

'Just leave me alone,' she choked, hugging her knees against her chest and burying her face in her arms. 'Please, leave me alone. Go and ring your actress.' She heard him swear under his breath.

'There is blood on your arm. You must have scraped it when you bumped into the doorframe. Let me look at it—'

'*Go away!*'

For a moment she thought he'd acceded to her request but then she heard the solid tread of his footsteps and he squatted down beside her, strong and calm, a man able to cope with any problem that came his way.

'You're going to make yourself ill. Enough.' Leandro slid his hands under her arms and lifted her to her feet and she looked up at him through eyes swollen with crying.

'Yes, it is enough.' Somehow she managed to get the words out. 'Enough pretending that our relationship can ever work. Enough pretending we can have any sort of marriage. It's over, Leandro. It's over.'

'You are *extremely* upset,' he breathed, holding her firmly so that she couldn't slide to the floor again, 'and it is never a good idea to make decisions when you're upset.'

'My decision is going to be the same whenever I make it. I mean it, it's over.' Her voice rose and he cupped her face in his hands, forcing her to look at him.

'Millie, I want you to take a deep breath.' His masculine voice was surprisingly gentle. 'Deep. That's right, and again. And now you are going to listen to me, yes? And you are going to trust me. Whatever is wrong—whatever has upset you this much—you will tell me and I will fix it. But for now I just want you to try and calm down.'

His unexpected kindness somehow made everything worse. 'Why won't you just leave me?'

'Because that option doesn't work for me,' he said grimly. 'I already told you, this time you are not walking away from our problems.' He drew her into his arms, but she shook him off and took a step backwards.

'Don't touch me. I can't bear you to touch me.' She heard the sharp intake of his breath and knew that her apparent rejection had hurt him.

'So you don't trust me.'

'This isn't about trust. This isn't about what happened with my sister. And it can't be fixed. Just—just—wait—and you'll see.' Her hands were shaking so much she couldn't untie the knot of silk holding together the edges of her robe and she almost screamed with frustration. Eventually the fabric loosened in her fingers and she bit her lip, trying to find the courage to do what she had to do. 'I don't know why you wanted me the first time, Leandro. You say I'm beautiful and—well, I never was. And even less so now.'

'I'm the best judge of that.'

'All right. Then judge.' Without giving herself any more time to think about it and change her mind, she allowed the dressing-gown to slip from her shoulders.

Naked, she faced him. Unprotected, she let him see. Vulnerable, she stayed silent and let him judge—*and saw his handsome face reflect everything she herself had felt over the past year.*

Shock, disbelief, distaste.

The emotions were all there.

'Now do you understand why I said this would never work? I wasn't beautiful enough for you before. How could I possibly be beautiful enough now?' Somehow the reality of exposing her damaged flesh was less traumatic than the thought of it had been. Now that she'd done it, she felt nothing but relief.

No more pretending.

He'd divorce her and she'd get on with her life. And it may not have been the life she'd dreamed off, but it would be all right. She'd make sure it was all right. She'd get over him, wouldn't she? It had only ever been a stupid dream.

Quietly sliding the robe back onto her shoulders, Millie cast one final look at his shocked face, reflecting on the fact she'd never actually seen him lost for words before.

'I'm sorry,' she muttered wearily. 'I'm sorry to do that to you—in that way. Perhaps it was cruel of me, but I honestly didn't…' Her pause was met with silence. 'I—just didn't know any other way.' Impulsively she lifted her hand to touch his arm and then realised that the best thing she could do for him was to just get out of his life.

Letting her hand drop, she walked past him towards the door feeling tired and completely drained of energy.

'God damn it, Millie, if you walk out on me one more time I won't be responsible for my actions.' His voice rasped across her sensitised nerve endings. 'You stay right there. I just need to—' He broke off and ran a hand over his face, clearly struggling with his emotions. 'Just give me a minute.'

She stopped walking. 'It doesn't matter. You don't need to work out what you're supposed to say or do. Nothing you say is going to make any difference.'

'Just *wait*.' Leandro pressed his fingers against the bridge of his nose and exhaled slowly. '*Maledezione,* you have no idea…'

'Yes, I do. I know what you're thinking. And I understand.'

'Do you?' His voice was harsh. 'Then you'll know that I'm asking myself what exactly I did to you that made you think you couldn't talk to me about this. Is this why you turned your back on me night after night?' He frowned and then shook his head, clearly angry with himself. 'No, of course. This…' He glanced towards her now concealed body. 'This didn't happen when we were together, did it? It couldn't have done. I would have known.'

Millie looked at him. 'It happened the day I left you.'

'*What* happened the day that you left me?' His hoarsely worded demand increased her tension.

'Can we talk about this tomorrow?' Seeing his face had been bad enough. She wasn't up to a conversation. She just wanted to hide.

Leandro gave a hollow laugh and his fingers closed around her wrist as he drew her firmly into the guest bedroom. 'No, *agape mou*. We're going to talk. Or perhaps I should say that *you're* going to talk. And you're going to do it now.'

CHAPTER EIGHT

KEEPING her hand in his, Leandro led her across the terrace
to the pool. The evening was still stiflingly warm and the
stylish curve of the swimming pool was illuminated by the
tiny lights that gleamed under the water.

'I always loved sitting out here at night,' she said softly,
sinking onto the edge of a sun lounger. 'It's so peaceful.'

'We made love out here. Do you remember?'

Millie didn't answer his question because she knew that
the only way she was going to be able to deal with the
present was if she didn't think about the past. 'So—what do
you want to know?'

He sat down right next to her, the length of his powerful
thigh brushing the length of hers. 'I want to know what
happened to you. I want to know how you got those scars.'
For once there was no mockery in his voice and she stared
down at their linked hands with almost curious detachment.

'When I drove away that day I was…' She hesitated. 'Very
upset. I didn't really think about where I was going. I drove
south and found myself in a very rough part of London. I
stopped at a set of lights—and three men took a fancy to the
car I was driving.'

His fingers tightened their grip on hers. 'Tell me.'

'Are you sure you want to hear it?'

'Yes.' But the word sounded as though it had been dragged from him and she looked up at his hard, set profile dubiously.

'If you're just going to rant and rave and turn all macho, this is going to be hard.'

'I won't rant and rave.'

'You promise not to go and extract revenge?'

Leandro made a sound that was close to a snarl. 'No,' he said thickly, placing her hand on his thigh and holding it there, 'no, *agape mou,* I don't make that promise.'

'Then—'

'What caused the scars?' he asked harshly. 'Was it a knife?'

'Broken bottle.' Millie felt the horror of it burst into her brain. 'Carjacking. I stopped at a set of lights—they had the doors open before I even saw them coming.'

'They dragged you out of the car?'

'I refused to undo the seat belt—big mistake. I think I was in a state of shock. But that resistance got me the scar on my stomach.'

The breath hissed through his teeth. 'Why didn't you just give them the keys?'

'You gave me the car as a wedding present,' she mumbled. 'I liked it.'

'Cars are replaceable.'

'Spoken like a billionaire.'

'I would say the same thing if I was living on benefits and someone had just stolen your bicycle.' He spoke in a low, urgent tone. '*Nothing* is worth that sort of risk.'

'Well, I suppose you don't really think clearly when it happens. You just react by instinct.'

'And you were upset and that was my fault.'

She stilled. 'You told me that you didn't have an affair with my sister.'

'I didn't. I'm blaming myself because I was so blisteringly angry that you didn't trust me, I let you walk out instead of dragging you back and proving my innocence to you. If I'd done that, this wouldn't have happened.' The breath hissed through his teeth again. 'Normally I'm not a believer in wasting time on regret but believe me, *agape mou,* when I say that with you, my regrets are piling up. But we'll deal with that in a minute. Finish the story. You were very badly injured?'

'Yes. They dragged me out of the car, attacked me with the bottle a few more times just to make sure I'd got the message and then took the car and my bag. I was unconscious, lying on the road—so I had no identity with me. I woke up days later in hospital with everyone wondering who I was. Initially they thought I was the victim of a hit and run.'

'Did you have amnesia?'

'No.' Millie shook her head. 'I remembered everything. They told me they'd found the car ten miles away, burned out and abandoned. Because no one had reported it missing, they hadn't been able to identify the owner. I was so angry with myself.' She frowned. 'I should have noticed them waiting at the lights.'

'You're not exactly streetwise.' Leandro toyed with her fingers. 'You hadn't even lived in a city until you married me. And on top of that, you were upset. Because of me.'

'You're not responsible for the carjacking. That was my own stupid fault for not locking my doors. But I wasn't used to London. Where I come from we wind the windows down and offer people lifts. People leave their front doors open.' Her frank confession drew a groan of disbelief from him.

'You are ridiculously trusting. And I'm angry with myself for not teaching you to be more careful.'

'*Not* your fault,' Millie said gruffly. 'Just another example of how I'm the wrong woman for you.'

'How can you reach that conclusion? It's becoming increasingly obvious to me that I had absolutely no idea what was going on in your head at any point during our short marriage. But we'll come back to that later. First I want you to finish telling me what happened.'

'I've told you everything.' Millie shrugged. 'I was in hospital for a while, obviously.'

'Why didn't the hospital contact me?'

'At first because I had no identity. And later…' She paused. 'Because I asked them not to.'

Leandro greeted that confession with a hiss of disbelief. 'Why would you do that? No, don't answer that.' His tone was weary. 'You thought I was having an affair with your sister. You thought she was pregnant with my child.'

'I thought our marriage was over.'

'Millie, we'd been together for less than three months and I couldn't get enough of you! Until you started turning your back on me, we were constantly together and it was good, wasn't it?'

'It was incredible. At first.'

'At first?'

'You worked very long hours. You were always jetting off to New York or Tokyo and you didn't want me with you.'

'Because I had trouble concentrating when you were around,' he bit out, and Millie looked at him in surprise because that explanation hadn't ever occurred to her.

'Oh.'

'Oh? What did you think the reason was?'

'I…wondered if you had other women.'

His jaw tightened. 'When, before that incident with your

sister, did I *ever* give you cause to doubt me?' Leandro released his grip on her hand and rose to his feet in a fluid movement. *'When?'*

'I suppose I looked at the facts. When I met you, you were thirty-two, rich, good-looking and single. You'd never been committed to a woman, but you'd been involved with plenty.'

'Before I met you.'

'And they were all different to me.'

Leandro spread his hands wide, his expression expectant. 'And does that tell you anything?'

'Yes. It tells me that you made a mistake when you married me.'

He sank his fingers into his hair and said something in Greek. 'Always if there are two ways to interpret something, you choose the wrong one.' His usually fluent English suddenly showed traces of his Mediterranean heritage. 'Did no other reason come to mind?'

Millie gave a tiny shrug. 'You're Greek.' At the moment there was no mistaking that fact. 'I was a virgin and you're old-fashioned enough to like that.'

His laugh lacked humour. 'Yes. All right. I concede that point. But I took your virginity within hours of meeting you so that wasn't a reason to marry you.'

'Well. Everyone makes mistakes,' she said simply. 'Even you.'

'Why didn't you contact me after the accident?'

'What for? If I couldn't hold you before I was injured, I knew there was no chance afterwards.' Millie stared at the still surface of the pool. 'And I knew I could never be the sort of wife you needed. Lying there in hospital gave me the time to think about that.'

'The sort of wife I needed? What is that supposed to

mean?' His tone raw, Leandro sat back down next to her. His hand slid under her chin and he forced her to look at him. '*You* were the woman I married. *You* were the wife I needed.'

'No.' Millie shook her head, tears swimming in her eyes. 'I wasn't, Leandro. I was *never* the wife you needed. I learned that pretty soon after we were married. We came back from our honeymoon and I was plunged into the life you lead— and nothing about the time we'd spent together had prepared me for what was expected of me.'

'Nothing was expected of you.'

'Oh, yes, people expected a lot.' The tears still glistening in her eyes, Millie moved her head away from the comfort of his fingers. 'You're Leandro Demetrios—declared the sexiest man in the world. Everyone wanted to know who you'd married. And everyone wanted to comment.'

'Who is everyone? Are you talking about the media?'

'Them, too. But mostly your friends. The people you mixed with in your daily life. They used to give me these little sideways glances that showed what they thought of your choice.'

'You were *my* wife,' he gritted. 'I didn't care what anyone thought of you.'

'But I did,' she said simply. 'I'm not like you. When they said I was fat and that my hair was curly, I cared. When they said I didn't dress like any of your previous girlfriends, I worried. They made me realise that I was totally wrong for you.'

Leandro growled low in his throat. 'And you didn't think I might have been the best judge of that?'

'I met one of your previous girlfriends.' She gave a twisted smile. 'She took great pleasure in drawing comparisons between herself and me. And she made the very apt comment that if she hadn't been able to hold you, how could I?'

'*When* did you meet her?'

'At a charity ball, the first week we spent in London. We were standing in front of the mirror together.' Millie nibbled her lip. 'I looked at what I was wearing and I looked at what she was wearing—well, let's just say I could see what she was talking about. I thought to myself, OK, so I need to dress differently. I treated it like a project. When I joined you at our table, I started studying everyone. And I got home and bought magazines, went shopping…'

'And so began your obsession with clothes. I had no idea.' His tone flat, Leandro gently rubbed her fingers with his. 'Those hours you spent in your dressing room every evening, trying on this dress and that dress—I thought you'd suddenly discovered the joys of shopping.'

'Joys?' Millie gave a hollow laugh. 'I hated it. Not that it isn't fun to have nice clothes, don't misunderstand me, but when you know that everything you wear is going to be criticised… Have you any idea how many clothes there are out there? How was I supposed to know what to wear? All I knew was that every time I went out, people stared at me. I just never seemed to get it right.'

'Why didn't you say something to me?'

'I presumed you could see for yourself,' she said wearily. 'And the fact that you were getting so impatient with me seemed to confirm that I was getting it all wrong.'

Leandro muttered something in Greek and rubbed his forehead with his fingers. 'We were at cross-purposes,' he said gruffly. 'I didn't think you were getting it wrong. I had no idea you were feeling like this.'

'I didn't know what looked good. Every time I thought I liked myself in something, I'd remember how many times I'd been wrong before. Then my sister rang and told me she needed somewhere to crash in London. You were away all the time—I thought she'd be company and I thought she'd be a good person to give me advice. She'd always helped me before. By then I was a mess,' she confessed. 'My confidence was on the floor. Everything I put on I found myself thinking, What are they going to say about this?'

'Why didn't you ask me if I liked what you were wearing?'

'Why didn't you just tell me?' Millie defended herself. 'On our honeymoon you seemed crazy about me—everything I wore, you stripped it off and made love to me. And then we arrived home and…you changed. And it took me a while to understand what was going on.'

'And what did you think was going on?'

'It was obvious. Our relationship was fine when we were here.' She waved a hand. 'Sort of like a holiday romance. But when it came to living your life, well, that's when the cracks appeared. And I panicked. I tried every outfit, every style— but I could see I was different to every other woman you'd ever been with. Every time we went out was torture. Everyone looked at me, judged me.'

Leandro swore under his breath. 'They didn't.'

'They did. People do it all the time. You don't notice because you don't care what people think of you.' Millie sneaked a glance at him. 'And you're not very tolerant of weakness in others. I remember one evening I begged you not to leave me with that group of women and you just frowned and told me I'd be fine. There was some government dignitary you had to speak to so you just threw me to the wolves and let them devour me.'

He winced. 'Millie—'

'It's all right, you don't have to say anything. The truth is you shouldn't have *had* to hold my hand at events like that. I was pathetic, I realise that, but every time we went out I was hit with another ten reasons why you shouldn't have married me and I was shocked by how nasty people were.'

'Why didn't you talk to me?'

'You were too absorbed in your work to notice what was going on. And you were already starting to get irritated with me. Your favourite trick was to glance at your watch and narrow your eyes when I was fumbling about, getting dressed. So I started getting ready earlier and earlier until in the end it took me most of the day. And then I'd appear and you'd be pacing the room like a caged tiger plotting his way out of captivity.'

'Waiting isn't my forte.'

'I noticed that. But from my point of view the fact that you were so irritated made the whole thing even more stressful. I would have spent most of the day getting ready and you'd look at me in disbelief as if you couldn't quite believe that was what I'd chosen to wear and then you'd usher me out to the car.'

'That is *not* what I would have been thinking,' Leandro muttered. 'I was probably thinking how much you'd changed. When first I met you, you didn't do any of those things. You were straightforward and lacking in vanity.'

'I'm sorry! That's because I had never been to a charity ball in my life! The highlight of my social calendar was the village fete.'

He raked his hands through his hair and gave a groan of frustration. '*That was a compliment, Millie!* Don't you ever hear a compliment?'

Stunned by the force of his tone, she looked at him in confusion. 'But you said— I thought—I thought lacking in vanity meant that I didn't spend hours on myself.'

'Yes, but you didn't *need* to spend hours on yourself. I

liked you the way you were. I liked you the way you were that day I first met you.'

'I was working on the farm! You arrived, designer dressed from head to toe, to talk business and I was wearing a pair of torn, ancient shorts and a T-shirt that had belonged to my dad but had shrunk in the wash.'

'I don't remember the shorts,' Leandro growled, 'but I do remember your legs. And your smile. And how sweet you were crawling over that haystack, risking life and limb to rescue those kittens that were trapped. I remember thinking, *I want her in my bed.* I want her looking after our babies. And I remember deciding at that moment that I wanted to wake up every morning looking at that smile. Why do you think I stayed two days? It was supposed to be a two-hour meeting.'

'You invested in my dad's business.'

Leandro gave a wry smile. 'I'm going to be honest here, *agape mou,* and confess that your dad's business is the only investment I've ever made that has lost me money.'

Millie gave an astonished laugh. 'You made a mistake?'

'No. I knew it was going to be a disaster the minute he showed me the numbers. I wasn't investing in the business. I was investing in you.'

She thought of the changes her dad had made to the farm. How excited he'd been by his new venture.

'Oh. It was kind of you to do that for Dad.' For a moment she was too flustered to respond, then she frowned slightly. 'But it doesn't change the fact that you didn't stop to think how I'd cope with it all, did you?'

Leandro took her hand again. 'I assumed you'd love the lifestyle. I knew your parents were struggling with the farm and you were working inhuman hours for a pittance.'

'But I didn't marry you for your money or the lifestyle,'

she said in a small voice. 'I married you for *you*. And you were always away being the big tycoon. And when we went out, there were always millions of people around us and I couldn't relax because there were cameras stuck in my face and everyone wanted to criticise me. Yes, I was lacking in vanity, but someone like that can't survive in your world. I hadn't realised just how much was involved in being a billionaire's wife. And those awful celebrity magazines tore me to pieces. At the beginning they said I was fat—or "full figured" was the exact phrase— And then I was in this column about fashion mistakes. Don't even *start* me on that one.'

'Why did you read them?'

'I thought it might help me work out what was expected of me. I wanted to look like the perfect wife.' She bit her lip. 'I wanted you to be proud of me. I didn't want you to sit there at a charity event thinking, Why did I marry her?

'I *never* thought that.'

'Didn't you?' Her smile was wan. 'I don't know. I just know that it got worse and worse. Until I no longer had the confidence to undress in front of you—until I couldn't bear the thought of having sex with you because I imagined that you must be thinking, Yuck, all the time. I just felt so self-conscious.'

'*Theos mou.*' His tone raw with emotion, Leandro rose to his feet and stood facing the pool, the muscles of his powerful shoulders flexing as he struggled for control. 'And I didn't see any of this. Never before have I considered myself to be stupid and yet obviously I am.'

'No. You just move in different circles to me. You take it all for granted. The women you dated before know how to do their hair, what to wear, how to talk, what to eat, how much they're supposed to weigh.'

'Who makes these rules?'

'Society.'

'And do you never break rules?'

'Sometimes.' Millie looked at him cautiously. 'But I was desperate not to embarrass you or make you ashamed.'

'Suddenly everything is falling into place.' Leandro spun to face her, his voice harsh. 'Why didn't you tell me you felt this way? Why not just have a conversation?'

'Telling your husband that you feel out of place and unattractive isn't the easiest conversation to have. I suppose part of me thought that if I said it aloud, I'd draw attention to it.' *As if he hadn't already noticed.* 'We had fundamental problems that no amount of words could fix. And after the accident, well, I knew I was going to have bad scars. The break in my leg meant that I was in hospital for ages. There was no way you would want to be with someone like me.'

'You reached that conclusion by yourself?' His tone was tight and angry and she felt her own tension increase.

'Yes. You're a man who demands perfection in every part of his life,' she said quietly, 'and I was so far from perfect. I was already insecure about how I was—the accident just made it all worse. Can't you see that?'

'What I see is that we left too many things unsaid. I also finally understand why you were so quick to condemn me when you saw me with your sister.' His voice was low and rough in the semi-darkness. 'Your own confidence was at such a low point that it didn't occur to you that I could be faithful to you. It seems as though you were resigned to the fact that I'd have an affair. You seemed to regard it as inevitable. You assumed that I would prefer your sister.'

Had she been wrong about that? For the first time ever a significant rush of doubt seeped into her brain. 'You and my sister—that was a much more obvious relationship than you and me.' *But she was starting to wonder.* 'Even if that hadn't happened then—with her—it would have happened eventually. Sooner or later some woman would have come along and caught your attention. Maybe you *did* find me attractive—but the novelty would have worn off. We weren't meant to be together, Leandro.' Millie pulled her robe more tightly around her. 'My accident just brought that home to me.'

'You've just made a great number of assumptions.'

'Did you come after me, Leandro?' Gently withdrawing her hand from his, she stood up. The soft lap of water against the side of the pool mingled with the sounds of the Mediterranean. In the distance she could hear the hiss of the sea on the sand, the chirping of the cicadas as they sang their night-time chorus. 'If you'd wanted me, you would have tracked me down. You're that sort of man. You go after what you want. And you didn't go after me.' *Whatever doubts might be in her head, that, at least, she was sure about.* 'Not even when my sister sent the baby to you.' She managed to keep the emotion out of her voice. 'I'm going to go to bed now. We can talk about what you want to do in the morning. Can I ask you one favour?'

His jaw tightened. 'Ask.'

'Whatever happened before is irrelevant. What matters is how things are now. Who I am now. You'll want to divorce me, and I understand that.' She stumbled over the words. 'But will you let me have custody of Costas? Whatever the will said, you have good lawyers and I'm his blood relative. I can't afford to fight for him.' She glanced at his face and saw the tension etched there. 'Just think about it.' And then she turned and walked back into the villa.

CHAPTER NINE

LEANDRO stood in the doorway of the guest bedroom, staring at the slight figure under the silk sheet.

She reminded him of an animal that had crawled away to die. And he knew she wasn't asleep.

She was hurt.

Because of him.

His tension mounted. Wasn't he the one who had told her that there was always more going on in a picture than first appeared? And had he taken his own advice? No. He'd seen and he'd judged.

And he knew why. No matter how distasteful it was to admit it, his own past had coloured the present. When she'd walked out…

Guilt, an unfamiliar emotion, clawed at his body but he thrust it away, knowing that regret would do nothing to fix the current situation.

So many words unspoken, he thought grimly, closing the door quietly and walking towards her. His bare feet made no sound on the cool tiles but he knew she'd heard him because he saw the defensive movement of her shoulders.

'I have lost count of the number of times you've turned

your back on me in our short marriage, Millie,' he said softly, 'and I allowed you to do it. But I'm not allowing it any more. Those days are over.'

'Go away, Leandro.' Her voice was muffled by the pillow and he saw her curl up just a little bit tighter, as if trying to make herself as small as possible.

This less than flattering response to his presence sent new tension through his already rigid frame. 'I'm not good at apologies,' he confessed, and then frowned as she curled up smaller still. 'But I know I owe you a big one.'

'You honestly don't have anything to apologise for. No man in their right mind would find me attractive.'

She thought he was apologising because he didn't find her attractive?

Stunned by her interpretation of his remark, Leandro struggled to find a suitable response and decided that, whatever he said, she wasn't going to believe him.

Abandoning words, he lay down on the bed next to her. He felt her shrink and saw her try and shift away from him but he placed his hand firmly on her hip, halting her slide to freedom. Used to negotiating himself out of difficult situations, it was a struggle to stay silent, but he knew that the time for slick verbal patter was long past. She'd made up her mind about herself and the way he saw her. Words weren't going to make a difference.

Applying a different tactic, Leandro slid his arm round her, drawing her rigid, defensive body against his. Through the thin silk robe he could feel her shivering and he frowned because the evening was hot and the air-conditioning in the unoccupied guest bedroom had been switched off. She wasn't cold. She was afraid.

Of him? *Of rejection?*

Taking unfair advantage of the differences in their physical strength, Leandro rolled her onto her back and shifted himself on top of her, his body trapping hers against the silk sheets.

'Why won't you leave me alone, Leandro?' Her voice was a broken plea and he stroked her damp, tangled hair away from her face with a gentle hand.

'I tried that,' he said softly. 'It was my biggest mistake.' Although there was just enough light shining in from the pool area for him to be able to make out the outline of her body, what was going on in her eyes was a mystery to him. He contemplated turning on the bedside light and then decided that it wouldn't be a good move. Maybe, this time, the dark would be helpful.

She tried to wriggle away from him but he was too heavy for her. 'Leandro, please. Don't do this.'

Leandro curved his hand around her cheek and drew her face back to his. He wanted desperately to see her expression. He also knew that if he turned that light on, her distress would stop him in his tracks.

'Don't do this, Leandro,' she whispered, trying to move her head.

Leandro silenced her plea with the warmth of his mouth. And what had begun as an attempt to silence her objections quickly turned into a sensual feast. With a groan, he deepened the kiss, wondering how he could have forgotten how good she tasted. She was strawberries and summer sunshine, honey and green English pastures. But, most of all, she was innocence. And he took ruthless advantage of her lack of sophistication, pushing aside the niggling thought that perhaps it wasn't entirely fair of him to use every erotic skill at his disposal when she was this emotionally vulnerable. They were past being fair, he reasoned, feeling a rush of satisfaction as her mouth moved under his, allowing him the access he was demanding.

Without breaking the kiss, he eased the sheet down her body and untied her robe one handed, careful to keep his movements slow and subtle. But slow and subtle could only take him so far, and he identified the exact moment she realised that he'd undone the robe because she suddenly stiffened under him.

Her arm lifted, but he anticipated her urge to cover herself and closed his fingers around her wrist. Drawing her arm above her head, he restrained her gently, feeling her tug against his grip as she tried to free herself. She writhed under him, the unconsciously sensual movement sending his blood pressure soaring. Just to be on the safe side, he drew her other arm above her head, holding both with one hand, leaving the other free to explore her quivering frame.

Leandro dropped his mouth to her throat, feeling her pulse pumping against the hot probe of his tongue. Her soft groan was half encouragement, half denial, and he gently moved her robe aside, exposing the soft curve of her breast.

She tugged at her wrists and he tightened his hold, feeling her instant response as he closed his mouth over the jutting pink tip of one swollen breast. Millie arched in an involuntary movement that brought her into direct contact with the hard thrust of his erection. Denying her feminine invitation, Leandro pressed her down against the bed with the power of his body, suppressing her attempts to relieve the sexual ache he'd created.

Soon, he promised himself. *Soon, he'd give her what she wanted. And himself too. But first…*

Dragging his tongue over the rigid peak of her nipple, he stroked his free hand over the flat, trembling planes of her

stomach, feeling the ridge of the scars under his seeking
fingers. He lingered for a moment, infinitely gentle—*did it
hurt?*—and then moved his hand lower still, this time to the
tops of her thighs. *Another scar here,* and he explored it with
the tips of his fingers and then shifted his weight to give
himself the access he wanted.

His fingers rested at the top of her thigh and he felt the tiny
movements of her pelvis as her body begged. Taking her
mouth again, he moved his hand, encountering soft curls,
damp now with the response he'd created. Stroking her gently,
he felt her gasp against his mouth and then the gasp turned
to a moan as he explored her intimately with sure, confident
fingers. She was warm and slick, and he took his time, using
all his skill and expertise to arouse her body past the point of
inhibition. Her moan of desperation connected straight to his
libido and suddenly it wasn't enough to touch. He wanted to
taste—all of her.

Easing his mouth from hers, Leandro looked down at her,
but he couldn't make out her features. Responding to her soft
moans, he released her hands, and this time she didn't move
them. She just kept them stretched above her head, like some
pagan goddess preparing herself for sacrifice.

Leandro slid down her quivering, sensitised body and
gently spread her thighs. He'd expected resistance, but her
eyes were still closed, her body compliant as he arranged her
as he wanted her and then lowered his head. The touch of his
mouth drew a soft gasp from her and he closed his hands
around her thighs, holding her still while he subjected her to
the most extreme sexual torture, his touch so gentle and impossibly skilled that he turned her from doubtful to desperate within seconds. The air was filled with her cries and he
continued his determined assault on her senses, sliding one

finger deep inside her, the feel of her slick femininity challenging his own control. His libido bit and fought but he continued to touch, stroke, taste until the excitement was a screaming force inside him and she was mindless and compliant under him.

Like a man clinging to a ledge with the tips of his fingers, Leandro refused to allow himself to fall, and then he felt her hands in his hair and on his shoulders.

'Now—Leandro, please…' Her broken plea was all he needed and he shifted over her, sliding his hand under the deliciously rounded curve of her bottom and lifting her.

He wanted to speak—*he wanted to tell her what he was feeling*—but he was afraid of anything that might disturb this fragile connection he'd created between them, so he stayed silent, rejecting the words that flowed into his brain, reminding himself that there would be time enough for talking later.

Her damp core was slick against the tip of his erection and he gritted his teeth in an effort to hold back and do this gently.

'Leandro…' Her hips thrust against him, the movement sheathing him sufficiently to rack up the sexual torture a few more notches. Keeping his weight on his elbows, he eased into her slowly, the sweat beading on his brow as he forced himself to take it slowly. Her body gripped his like a hot, tight fist and his reacted by swelling still further, drawing a gasp from her parted lips.

'Leandro…'

'It's all right,' he breathed, 'just relax—your body knows how to do this. Relax, *agape mou,* and trust me.' He licked at her lips, nibbling gently, coaxing and teasing until he felt her respond. But he didn't move, holding himself still until she moved her hips in a tentative invitation.

By a supreme effort of will, Leandro held onto control,

keeping his own ravenous libido in check as he waited for her to reach the same point of desperation.

Millie groaned his name, arched and shifted, but still he didn't move, the muscles in his shoulders pumping up and hard under the effort of holding back. Only when she sobbed out a plea and rubbed her thigh along the length of his did he allow himself to move again, and this time her body drew him in deep, her slick delicate tissues welcoming the hard thrust of his manhood.

Trying to think clearly through the red mist that clouded his brain, Leandro slid one hand down her thigh, urging her to wind her legs around him, and then adjusted his own position in a decisive movement that drew a soft gasp from her.

Her soft moans increased with each rhythmic thrust and he was so aware of every movement she made that he felt the exact moment when her body tumbled out of control. The ecstatic tightening of her body stroked the length of his erection and he finally lost his own grip on control and fell with her, joining her in that scorching, exhilarating, terrifying rush to the very edges of extreme pleasure.

His mind blanked. In those few moments of exquisite perfection he forgot everything except the amazing chemistry that he created with this woman.

And as the sizzling, vicious response of his body finally calmed, he became aware of two things. One, that she was no longer fighting him and, two, that he was still hard.

Which gave him a choice.

He could either withdrew and allow her to sleep, or he could do what his body was urging him to do.

Allowing himself a half-smile in the safety of the darkness, Leandro made his choice.

* * *

Millie stared at herself in the bathroom mirror, seeing wild hair and flushed cheeks. And that was hardly surprising, was it? He'd made love to her until dawn.

Until dawn...

Trying to ignore the hurt that bloomed inside her, she pulled on a pair of loose trousers and a simple T-shirt and walked out onto the terrace.

A lizard lay basking in the heat of the sun and, nearby, one of the cats was stretched out, slowly licking his fur.

And as relaxed as any of them was Leandro, lounging at the breakfast table with his legs stretched out, his gaze focused on the financial pages of a newspaper. A coffee cup lay empty next to his lean, bronzed hand, his dark hair still damp from the shower.

Millie cleared her throat and he glanced up. His slow, sure smile made her want to hit him.

Leandro the conqueror, she thought miserably. *Man enough to bed a woman even when he didn't find her attractive.*

'*Kalimera.*' He greeted her in Greek. '*Te kanis?* How are you?'

'I'm fine, thank you.'

His eyes narrowed instantly and Millie quivered with suppressed emotion, so utterly humiliated that if she'd been able to leave the island without speaking to him, she would have.

She didn't want to have this conversation, but she knew that Leandro was far too quick not to pick up on her distress.

He folded the newspaper carefully and put it to one side. 'Obviously you're not feeling so good this morning.'

'I'm fine.'

'Fine?' His eyes rested on hers and then he said something in Greek to the staff who were hovering. They melted away, leaving the two of them alone on the terrace. 'All right.' His tone was even. 'We no longer have company. You can tell me what you think of me.'

'You don't want to know.'

'Yes,' he said softly, 'I do. No more secrets, remember?'

'All right.' Millie curved her hand over the back of the chair, too wound up and upset to contemplate joining him at the table. 'If you really want to know what I think—I think you are the most ruthless, insensitive man I've ever met.'

Stunned dark eyes met hers. 'Run that past me again?'

'You heard me.'

'I presume this interesting sentiment has hit you in the cold light of day. It certainly wasn't what was going through your mind last night when you were naked and sobbing in my bed.'

'Don't speak like that! I find it *really* embarrassing. It's bad enough that you do all those things to me and make me—you know…' Hot colour flooded her cheeks and she looked away from his hot gaze, unable to look him in the eye and maintain the conversation. 'It's as if you're sitting there smugly congratulating yourself on your amazing ability to turn any woman to jelly no matter what What were you trying to prove?'

Leandro was unusually still, his gaze partially concealed by thick, black lashes. 'What makes you think I was trying to prove something?'

'Because why else would you have devoted your night to that whole…' Millie waved her hand wildly '…seduction routine. What? *What was it all about?*'

'They say actions speak louder than words—didn't last night say anything to you?'

'Yes. It said that you didn't know how to apologise, but you do know how to have sex.'

'You think that was apology sex?'

'I'd rather think that than the alternative.'

'Which is?'

'Pity sex. That's far worse than apology sex.'

'You think I made love to you because I felt sorry for you? I'm not sure the male anatomy would allow "pity sex", whatever that is.' His apparent lack of emotion somehow made everything worse.

'I'm sure yours would—you don't exactly have a problem with your sex drive, do you? Although I did notice that even you had to do it in the dark.'

'"Do it"?' He repeated her words with careful emphasis, the subtle lift of one eyebrow reminding her of just how unsophisticated she was compared to him.

Millie rubbed her damp palms on her loose trousers, wishing she hadn't started this conversation. 'It wasn't making love. Making your point would be closer to the mark. Why did you do it? Was it a challenge to your reputation as the ultimate lover? Or was it supposed to be a going-away present? You don't want me to feel bad about myself so you decided to give me a good night before you sent me packing, is that right?' Her emotions were in such a heightened state of turbulence that his calm, watchful gaze was even more infuriating. 'Aren't you going to say something?'

Leandro stirred and drew in a breath. 'I only realised yesterday how insecure you are, and clearly I've underestimated the depths of that insecurity.' Putting his napkin carefully down on the table, he stood up.

Something in the set of his powerful shoulders and the glint in his eye made her step backwards but he was too quick for her. His hand closed around her wrist and when she twisted it in an attempt to free herself he simply drew her closer.

Memories of the way he'd held her hands in the moonlight

deepened the flush on her cheeks. Hope warred with her feelings of inadequacy.

'Let me go. You're always grabbing me! What do you think you're doing?'

'You think last night was all about pity sex—you think I'm only capable of only "doing it" in the dark.' He swung her into his arms, strode a few paces across the terrace. 'Well, it's not dark now, *agape mou,* so let's test that theory, shall we?'

'Put me down, Leandro!'

He lowered her onto the nearest sun lounger. 'I've put you down.' His voice was a soft dangerous purr and he undid the clasp of her trousers with a practised flick of his fingers.

With a gasp of shock she clutched at her trousers but she was too late. They were already discarded on the floor and his hands were stripping off her T-shirt with the same decisive force. 'Stop it. Leandro, what are you *thinking?*'

'That you're incredibly sexy,' he growled, releasing the catch on her bra and stripping off her panties without pause or hesitation. It was easy for him, with his vastly superior strength, to keep her where he wanted her. 'And I'm thinking that being thoughtful wasn't the right approach. Apparently what a man sees as sensitive, a woman can see as insensitive.'

Horribly conscious of the sun blazing a spotlight onto her naked body, Millie tried to slither away from him but Leandro held her firmly, a dangerous gleam in his eyes. 'No more hiding, *agape mou.* No more robes, long trousers or dark rooms. We will do this in daylight and then you will know the truth, *hmm?* You will see how sorry I feel for you—how this injury of yours has affected me. You want to know if I'm aroused? If you still turn me on? Let's see, shall we?'

'Don't do this.' Millie drew her knees up, trying to cover

herself but he pushed her legs down with one hand and deftly dealt with the zip of his trousers with the other.

'Do I look as though I'm having a problem becoming aroused, *agape mou?* Do I look like a man doing you a favour?' His eyes glittered as he dispensed with his trousers, boldly unselfconscious as he stripped himself naked, exposing his lean, bronzed body. Lean, bronzed, *aroused* body.

With the flat of his hand Leandro pushed her gently back against the sun lounger and came over her in a fluid movement that was all dominant male.

His muscles were pumped up and hard and she felt the brush of his chest hair against the sensitised tips of her breasts.

When the blunt tip of his erection brushed against her exposed thigh she gave a gasp of shock that turned to a moan as he buried his face in her neck.

'Does that feel like pity?' He moved against her boldly and Millie groaned and turned her head away because the sudden explosion of excitement that consumed her was just too humiliating.

'Don't do this, Leandro…'

'Why? Because you're afraid I'm doing it because I feel sorry for you? I never do things for other people, *agape mou,* you should know that by now. I'm selfish. I do things for myself. Because it's what I want.' His tone rough, he took her hand and drew it down to that part of himself, and her mouth dried because he was velvety hard and she could barely circle him with her shaking fingers. 'I know you had no experience before I met you,' he purred, 'so let me spell out the facts, *pethi mou.* This isn't called pity. It's called chemistry. Hot, sexual chemistry. It isn't me "making my point", as you so eloquently put it, it's me making love.' He caught her face in his hands and lowered his mouth to hers. 'Making love,' he said against her lips. 'Have you got that?'

'Leandro—'

'I want you. I've always wanted you and that isn't going to change. Are you listening?' He slid his hand behind her neck and forced her to hold his gaze. 'Are you listening to me?'

Her hand was still holding him and she stared into the fierce heat of his eyes and forgot everything except the burning need in her pelvis.

His hand slid under her bottom, shifting her position. 'You have scars on your body, yes,' he said thickly, 'but it's still your body. One day, when you have my babies, you might have stretch marks or maybe other scars, but this will still be your body. And it's *your* body that I want. No other woman's.'

Babies?

Her head was spinning, her pulse racing out of control as she struggled to hold onto her thoughts before they slipped away. He'd said— Had he said…?

While she was struggling with his words, he entered her with a determined thrust, sliding deep, and Millie gave up on any thought of responding because the feel of him inside her drove every coherent thought from her brain. Unprepared for his invasion, she tried to make a sound but his mouth closed over hers and he held her hips as he drove deeper still, his virile thrust taking him straight to the heart of her. This time there was no gentle foreplay, no slow, clever strokes of his long fingers. Just an unapologetic demonstration of raw sexuality and male dominance.

His hand locked in her hair, Leandro lifted his head just enough to allow him to speak. 'Can you feel me, Millie?' He growled the words against her lips and ground deeper inside her. 'Can you feel me inside you?' He was big, hard and shockingly male, and she sobbed his name and dug her nails into his back, her body so sensitised by his invasion that she could hardly breathe. In that moment she'd never felt so wanted, truly desired.

His breathing unsteady, he gently bit her lower lip and then soothed it with his tongue. 'You feel incredible,' he murmured huskily, and he withdrew slightly and her eyes flew wide.

'No…'

'No what?' He gave a slow, wicked smile, withdrawing still further. 'No, don't stop—or, no, don't do this?'

'Leandro…'

He kept her on the edge for several agonising seconds and then slid deep again, the movement sending shock waves of excitement through her trembling frame.

'This isn't pity sex,' he breathed, lifting her hips to allow him even, 'it's hot sex, *agape mou*. It's what you and I share. Can you feel it?'

Millie was incapable of speech, her body rushing forward to meet the pleasure that he was creating with each skilled, fluid stroke. For a delicious moment her eyes met his. He held that look, the connection between them impossibly intimate. And then everything inside her splintered apart and she arched her back as her body was convulsed by an erotic explosion so intense that she couldn't catch her breath. The sensations devoured her, tearing through her body like a ravenous beast on the rampage, and she felt the sudden tension in his body and the increase in masculine thrust that brought him to the same dizzying peak of hot liquid pleasure.

Millie lay in dazed, breathless silence for a moment, her mind incapable of functioning. She was dimly aware of the hot sun burning her leg and the roughness of his thigh against her more sensitive flesh. And then she heard the distant buzz of a motorboat somewhere in the distance and was suddenly hideously conscious of the fact they were naked.

'Leandro…' She pushed against his bare shoulder, suddenly panicking that someone was going to see them. 'We have to move.'

'Why?' Typically relaxed, he raised himself onto his elbow and surveyed her from under thick, dark lashes. 'What's the hurry?'

'Your staff—'

'Don't venture near my private terrace,' he said smoothly, dropping a lingering kiss to her parted lips.

'But what if one of them comes to clear up the breakfast things?'

'I'll fire them.' He kissed her cheek. 'Relax.'

But she couldn't relax. 'I should check Costas.'

'He has a nanny, remember? And if he was awake you would have heard him through the baby alarm.'

'What if it isn't working? I need to get dressed, Leandro.'

'No. You don't. You just want to hide your body and I'm not going to let you.'

'You may be comfortable with nudity, but that's only because you look great.'

'Thank you.' Laughing, he caught her face in his hands. 'You have a great body, too. I thought I'd just proved that. You're *not* running away.'

Millie bit her lip and then gave a faltering smile. 'I really do want to see the baby. It's been such an upheaval for him, being passed around as if he's some sort of trophy. He needs stability and security. I want him to know I'm here. I need to take a shower and dress.'

He sighed and lowered his mouth to hers. 'You are quite extraordinary,' he murmured softly, stroking her hair back from her face. 'Go on, then. I'll see you in a minute.'

Her senses and emotions churning from what had happened between them, she drew away from him and walked awkwardly across the terrace and back into the bedroom.

Locking herself in the bathroom, she turned on the shower, wondering what exactly had it all meant to him. What had he been proving? Convinced that he'd made love to her in the night out of some misplaced sense of guilt, she was no longer sure of anything. Not even herself. Her body still ached and tingled from their lovemaking and she stepped under the shower and then changed into a long cotton skirt and a strap top.

She contemplated blow-drying her hair and decided against it, anxious in case Costas had woken and was upset.

Hurrying along to his room, she heard happy gurgles and cooing and walked in to find him lying in Leandro's arms.

Millie watched for a moment, her insides turning to mush as she saw how gentle he was with the baby. He was speaking in soft, lyrical Greek and then he looked up and saw her.

'And here is beautiful Millie.' He placed a kiss on top of the baby's head and handed him over. 'He seems quite happy.'

Millie took the baby, feeling his solid warmth in her arms. 'He needs his nappy changed.'

'Now, *that*,' Leandro drawled, 'is definitely outside my area of expertise. Do you want me to call the nanny?'

'Believe it or not, I'm capable of changing a nappy.' Millie laid Costas on a changing mat on the floor. Relieved to have a reason to avoid Leandro's disturbing gaze, she cooed at the baby who kicked his legs in delight. 'He thinks I can't change a nappy.'

'Why don't you put him on the bed?'

'Because he might roll off.' Millie deftly changed the nappy and scooped the baby against her. 'Time for breakfast.'

'Give him his bottle on the terrace,' Leandro instructed. 'There are things I want to say to you.'

She looked at him warily. 'Things that can be said in front of a baby?'

He looked amused. 'Absolutely. In the unlikely event that he files our conversation for future reference, it will do him good to know that adults can sort out their problems rather than giving up on their marriage. That is the example I would want to set for the younger generation. And you?'

Millie's heartbeat faltered. 'I— We— It isn't that simple, Leandro—you're unrealistic.'

He guided her towards the door that led to the vine covered terrace. 'The difference in our approach may be rooted in our cultures. Your divorce rate is higher than ours.'

Still holding Costas, Millie sighed as she walked towards the table that had been set for breakfast. 'I think cultural differences are the least of our problems at this point in our relationship.'

His response to that was to turn and deliver a slow, confident smile. 'Problems are merely there to test resolve. If you really want something, you can overcome the problems.' He stepped towards her, closing the gap until she drew in a breath. 'How much do you want our marriage to work, Millie?'

How much? Her heart was thudding and she was trapped by the unshakable confidence in his eyes. 'I—I want it, of course, but you don't—'

'Don't I?' He didn't even wait for her to finish the sentence. 'What do you think this morning was all about?'

'I have no idea. I'm assuming your caveman tendencies ran a little out of control.'

The look in his eyes sent her pulse racing again and she stepped backwards, grateful that she was holding the baby.

'I need to feed Costas.'

'If you think that's going to get you off the hook, you don't know me. We're going to talk about this, *agape mou*. I'm going to explore every last corner of…' His voice tailed off and her breathing quickened because the look in his eyes was unmistakably sexual.

'Of?'

His smile widened. 'Of our relationship,' he purred, and she knew he was perfectly aware that she'd been waiting for him to say 'your body.'

Millie gritted her teeth and was about to stalk towards the table when he closed his hand over her shoulder and bent his head so that his mouth was by her ear.

'That, too,' he murmured silkily, and the colour flooded into her cheeks.

'You've done enough exploring for one day.'

'I haven't even started.' Leandro pulled the chair out for her and made sure she had what she needed for the baby. Then he took the seat opposite her and poured her some coffee.

'What was it you wanted to say to me?' The anticipation of the conversation to come scraped at her insides like sandpaper, putting her off her food. Trying to distract herself, she slid the teat into the baby's mouth, her expression softening as he clamped his jaws and started to suck.

'Eat some food. This honey comes from a friend's bees. It's delicious.'

'I'm not hungry.'

'Eat, or I will feed you,' he said pleasantly, but his eyes glinted warningly across the table. 'I overlooked the fact that you didn't eat last night. You'd worked yourself up into a state

about telling me what had happened to you, and you'd braced
yourself for rejection. But that didn't happen, did it, Millie?
You are still sitting at my table, having just climbed out of
my bed—metaphorically at least—so there is no longer a
reason for you to have lost your appetite.'

'Nothing's changed, Leandro.' She watched as he drizzled
the thick, golden honey over the creamy yoghurt. 'The issues
between us are still there.'

'All right—so let's address those issues because the worry
is affecting you badly. First, can I get you anything? This
sweet pastry is delicious.'

Millie shook her head, envying his calm. 'You're not
stressed, are you?'

'What is there to be stressed about?' He drank his coffee
and replaced the cup carefully in the saucer. 'I am relaxing
on a beautiful island with a beautiful woman. If I found that
stressful, I would be a fool, no?'

She closed her eyes briefly. 'So you're just going to
pretend that sex solves everything.'

'No. I'm not going to pretend that. I want to make a few
things clear to you. I made love to you in the dark last night
because you were clearly very upset and I thought it was the
sensitive thing to do, but…' he gave a self deprecating smile
'…as I now know, a man's idea of what is sensitive isn't
always the same as a woman's. As you keep pointing out, I'm
not that good at the whole sensitive side of things, so I need
to work on that.'

Millie gave a strangled laugh. 'What? You're suddenly
going to turn into a modern man?'

'I wouldn't go that far.' There was humour in his tone and
in the glance he sent in her direction. 'Tell me why you think
I made love to you in the dark?'

'Isn't it obvious?' *Was he going to make her spell it out?*

Apparently he was, because he showed no inclination to let her off the hook. 'I think we've both accepted that what is obvious to me isn't obvious to you and vice versa. Guessing games haven't done much for the success of our relationship to date.'

Unable to argue with that, Millie grimaced. 'All right.' She adjusted the bottle in the baby's mouth. 'You made love to me in the dark because you didn't want to see my body. I thought being in the dark was the only way you could be sure you'd be able to—' She broke off and his eyes gleamed with sardonic humour as he challenged her unspoken assumption.

'Well, you were wrong about that, weren't you?'

Remembering just *how* wrong, her mouth dried. 'I suppose I was.'

His mind clearly lingering on the same memories, he gave a slow, masculine smile. 'It was fantastic, no?'

Millie looked away from him. 'It didn't solve anything.'

'Yes, it did.' His voice soft, Leandro leaned across the table and took her hand. 'It told me a great deal about you.'

'That I'm easy?'

'Easy?' He gave a hollow laugh. 'You're the most difficult woman I know. In every sense. You're complicated, contrary, you don't say what you think—and you put thoughts in other people's heads.' He paused. 'And that brings us to the most important part of this conversation.'

'Which is what?'

'Your insecurities. We married quickly, as you constantly remind me.' He pulled a face. 'And I didn't take the time to get to know you properly. That was my first mistake. The sex overwhelmed us both, I think.'

'Yes, it did. You can't build a marriage on…' she cast a

worried look at the baby and lowered her voice '…sex. Sex isn't communication.'

'Actually, I disagree.' His gaze was direct. 'I think sex is often a very honest form of communication. On our honeymoon you were insatiable—affectionate, uninhibited and spontaneous. When you turned your back on me, I should have made you talk. Instead, I gave you space.' Leandro leaned back in his chair. 'You assumed that I'd prefer your sister to you, isn't that right?'

'Yes.' Millie didn't lie. 'Becca was beautiful, elegant and witty. She wouldn't have had any difficulties knowing what to wear and what to say.'

'So you saw us together and instead of thinking, *He wouldn't,* you thought *I understand why he would.*'

'Sort of.'

'So would you agree that the whole incident said more about you than it did about me?'

Her heart was thumping. *Had she been unfair?* The doubt was slowly growing in her mind. 'Maybe. I don't know. She was my sister.' She bit her lip. 'I just want to put the whole thing behind us.'

His mouth tightened for a moment and then he lifted a padded envelope from the table and handed it to her. 'This is for you.'

'What is it?' Millie slid her hand into the packet and withdrew some discs. 'What are these?'

'It's the CCTV footage of what happened in the pool that day. Take it.' He leaned forward. 'It proves that I'm telling the truth.'

'You had proof?'

'I have a very sophisticated security system in the house.'

'But you didn't show me before?'

Leandro hesitated. 'Two reasons,' he said softly. 'Firstly,

because I had this idealistic wish for my wife to have unques
tioning faith and trust in me. Secondly, I didn't want to be th
one who exposed your sister for what she was. I'm doing i
now because I realise how insecure you are and I don't wan
you to feel that way.'

Her heart lifted and sank and Millie looked at him help
lessly. 'So this proves my husband is innocent and my siste
is guilty.'

'Yes.'

Struggling with the truth, she fingered the CDs. 'Whe
Becca came to stay, I thought she was helping me. But sh
was targeting you, wasn't she?'

'I think we have to assume that.'

Reflecting on that, Millie bit her lip and then put the CD
back in the envelope. 'Thanks,' she said gruffly, 'for giving
me the chance to see them. Now I'm the one who owes you
an apology.'

'Aren't you going to look at them?'

'No.' Millie rubbed her fingers over the envelope. 'I believe
you. I think perhaps a small part of me always believed you
but believing you meant accepting that Becca—' She broke
off and Leandro breathed out heavily.

'I know. I'm sorry.'

'She was my family. Someone I trusted.' Millie lifted her
eyes to his and saw dark shadows there. 'What? You think I
was stupid to trust her?'

'No.' His voice was rough. 'You should be able to trust
family. It's just that sometimes…' He muttered something
under his breath and stood up abruptly. 'Enough of this
Millie. It's in the past now.'

Millie looked at him, wondering what was going on in his
mind. 'Leandro—'

'I want you to forget it,' he ordered. 'I want to put it behind us.'

'But it doesn't really change the facts! You need a wife who's able to stand by your side at glittering functions, someone who can hold her own with the elite of Hollywood, politicians, businessmen—'

'And I have a wife capable of all those things. The only thing she apparently isn't capable of is believing in herself.' Leandro reached for her hand across the table. 'But that is going to change.'

'I appreciate what you're trying to do, but you have to be realistic. That actress was right—I'm not your type.'

'She was trying to destroy your confidence.' His fingers tightened on hers. 'Are you going to let her?'

'Very possibly.' Millie gave a weak smile. 'You think I should look in the mirror and say I'm more beautiful than her? I'd have to be treated for hallucinations.'

Leandro gestured to a staff member who was hovering discreetly, and she hurried up and carefully lifted Costas from Millie's arms.

'I don't want him corrupted,' Leandro said silkily, 'so I didn't think he should be here for the next part.' He stood up and drew her against him intimately, a smile playing around his firm mouth. 'Are you aware of your own power yet?'

Feeling the hard thrust of his arousal, she looked at him in amused disbelief. 'You're insatiable.'

'With you, yes. You turn me on,' he breathed, lowering his mouth to hers, 'and on, and on. All the time. And I want you, all the time. So next time you don't feel beautiful, remind yourself of that.'

'So what happens now?'

'You learn to be yourself. No more dressing as you think

you are expected to dress—no more behaving as you are expected to behave. Just be you. Is that so hard?'

'And when I embarrass you?'

Leandro smiled. 'That won't happen. I find you beautiful, generous and kind and I intend to devote the next few weeks to making you believe in yourself.'

If they could have stayed in Greece forever, maybe their relationship would work, Millie thought. But his life was so much bigger than this one, idyllic island.

And what was going to happen then?

CHAPTER TEN

THE idyll lasted two more weeks.

'He loves his afternoon nap. He's sleeping really well now.' Millie tucked Costas into the cot and tiptoed towards Leandro, who was waiting in the doorway. He was dressed casually in shorts and a polo shirt and his dark hair gleamed in the sunshine.

'You are very good with him.' His eyes lingered on her face. 'And extremely generous to give so much of yourself to a child who isn't yours.'

Millie was horribly conscious of his scrutiny. 'He's part of my sister.'

Leandro took her hand and led her across the terrace and towards the narrow path that led down through a garden of tumbling Mediterranean plants to the beach. 'You are nothing like her.'

'I'm well aware of that. My parents were constantly reminding me of that.'

Leandro frowned down at her. 'Really?'

'I don't blame them. I never gave my parents anything to boast about. I was never top in maths, I was only ever picked for the netball team if everyone else was struck down by some vile virus or other, I didn't play a musical instrument,

I have a voice like a crow with a sore throat and I don't have the face and body of a model.'

'And is all that important?'

'Among you alpha high achievers, it is. My mum's face glowed with pride when she introduced Becca to anyone— "This is my daughter who works as a top model but she also has a maths degree from Cambridge, you know." And then she'd turn to me and say, "And this is our other daughter— Millie isn't academic, are you dear?" And I'd feel the same way I felt when I got my spelling wrong at school. The teachers would sigh and say, "You're nothing like your sister, are you?" as if that was a major disadvantage in life.'

'No wonder you have no confidence. But all that is going to change.' As they reached the bottom of the path, Leandro tightened his grip on her hand. 'You can't possibly still be feeling insecure,' he murmured, taking her face in his hands and kissing her. 'For the past two weeks we've done nothing but talk and make love.'

'Maybe I'm having problems believing that anyone can be this lucky,' Millie replied humbly, wrapping her arms around his neck. 'And I still can't believe you don't want someone who you can discuss the money markets with over breakfast.'

'I can't think of anything more guaranteed to put me off my food.' He dragged his thumb across her mouth in an un- mistakably sensual gesture. 'I work in a very high-pressured, conflict-ridden environment—when I come home I don't want to discuss work. And I don't want conflict. I want a soft, warm woman who can challenge me in other ways. Which you do. So the answer to your unspoken question, *agape mou,* is no. I didn't ever want your sister. But I have told you that before.' He released her and took her hand, leading her towards the jetty.

Millie looked at the sleek motorboat. 'We're going out on that?'

'I feel in need of an adrenaline rush,' he drawled. 'In the absence of anyone to fire, bully or intimidate, I need to find alternative forms of excitement.'

Her eyes slid to his and he gave a slow grin. 'Yes, we'll be doing that, too,' he purred, helping her into the boat and loosening the rope. Lithe and agile, he followed her into the boat, taking the control with his usual cool confidence. 'Do you get seasick?'

'I don't know, but I'm probably about to find out.' Her nerve endings sizzling from the chemistry that constantly flared between them, she tried to concentrate. 'How fast are you going to go?'

His smile widened. 'Fast.'

And he did.

Having eased the boat skilfully out of the shallow bay, he pushed the throttle forwards and sent the boat flying across the waves at a speed that took her breath away.

Millie held tight to the seat, meeting his brief, questioning glance with an exaggerated smile of delight.

Men, she thought, relieved that she hadn't bothered with a hat. Her hair flew around her face and the spray from the waves stung her cheeks.

Leandro kept up the pace until they reached a neighbouring island, and then he cut the engine and dropped the anchor.

'Presumably you could have gone at half the pace.'

'And that would have taken twice the time.' Unapologetic, he leaned forward and kissed her hard. 'I don't like hanging around.'

'I'd noticed.' Millie looked towards the beach. 'Is that where we're going?'

'Later. If you want to. First I want to show you something. Put this on.' He handed her a slim, expensive-looking box with a discreet logo in the corner, which she recognised as that of a top fashion designer.

'If this is another swimming costume, you can forget it. In the last ten days all you've done is make me take my clothes off all the time.'

'That isn't quite all I've done, *agape mou.*'

She blushed. 'OK, so I wore a swimming costume on your island, but presumably this isn't private. Anyone could see me.'

"You have nothing to hide.'

'I still can't believe you got me into a swimming costume.'

'You looked fabulous.'

'From the back.'

'Yes, from the back. And from the front. And the side. From every angle,' Leandro said, sliding his shorts off to reveal the strong, flat stomach and hard thighs. 'You seem a little overdressed for a Greek beach. Open the box.'

'Where did this come from, anyway? You haven't been anywhere to buy me anything.'

He spread his hands in masculine apology. 'All right—I confess I didn't actually choose it. I made a call, gave someone a brief and it was delivered.'

'You made a call.' She mimicked him as she opened the box. Wrapped carefully inside layers of luxurious silken tissue paper was the sexiest bikini she'd ever seen. It was a shimmering gold and she could see that it was brief enough to be virtually non-existent. Her heart thudded uncomfortably. 'No *way,* Leandro!'

'Put it on.'

'I can't possibly wear this.'

'Trust me, you will look sensational in it.' Calm and unconcerned, he stripped off his T-shirt, revealing bronzed shoulders hard with muscle. 'I will enjoy watching you change into it.'

'Leandro.' Her tone was urgent and her fingers tightened on the slippery fabric. 'A swimming costume—well, I managed that. But I can't wear a bikini. I just can't. I have—'

'Scars—yes, I know.' He was as relaxed as she was agitated, and her fingers tightened on the silky fabric.

'You don't understand how self-conscious I feel.'

'I understand *exactly* how self-conscious you feel and I am trying to show you that I find you incredibly sexy in whatever you're wearing.' His voice was husky. 'Or *not* wearing. Get changed.'

Millie held the bikini in her hands. Looked at it. Then she saw the determination in his eyes. 'I can't wear a bikini.'

'You have ten seconds to change,' he warned in a silky tone, 'or I will put it on you myself.'

'You're not very sympathetic, are you?'

'Do you want my sympathy?'

'No. I just want to hide and you won't let me. For the past two weeks you've done nothing but expose me! You make love in daylight, you make me parade around in a swimming costume and now this.'

Leandro glanced pointedly at his watch. 'You're down to one second. Are you going to do it yourself or do I do it for you?'

Sending him a furious glare, Millie snatched up one of the neatly folded towels and retreated to the far side of the boat. Was he being intentionally cruel? Angry and upset, she wriggled into the minuscule bikini, snatched her clothes up from the baking leather of the seat and stalked back to him.

'Satisfied?'

'Not yet.' His smile was wickedly sexy as his eyes trailed down her body. 'But I will be. Remind me to thank the person who chose that. She followed my brief exactly. The emphasis being on the word "brief".'

Flustered by his lazy, masculine scrutiny, Millie stared down at the clear water. Shoals of tiny silvery fish darted beneath the surface and she watched them for a moment. 'I don't understand you.'

'Evidently not. But we're working to change that. You look fantastic in that bikini.'

She opened her mouth to argue with him but he walked across to her, wrapped his arms around her and kissed her. The heat he created with his mouth eclipsed anything produced by the sun, and Millie felt her body melt and her mind shut down. She forgot that she wanted to cover herself. She forgot to feel self-conscious. Instead, she felt beautiful and seductive.

When he finally lifted his head, she felt dizzy. 'How is your confidence now?'

Basking in the sexual appreciation, she gave a reluctant smile. 'Recovering.'

'Good. Because we are flying back to London tomorrow.'

Millie felt as though she'd been punched in the stomach. 'Why?'

'Because my business demands it,' he said dryly, stroking her hair away from her face. 'I have been absent for a long time—there are things that need my attention. And tomorrow night we have a gala evening to attend.'

'Tomorrow?' Millie tensed. 'You haven't given me any warning!'

'I didn't want you turning yourself into a nervous wreck.'

'Who will be there?'

'I will be there.' Leandro released his hold on her and stepped onto the side of the boat. 'And I am the only person that matters in your life.' With that arrogant statement, he executed a perfect dive, his lean, bronzed body slicing into the water with powerful grace.

Millie stared after him in frustration, realising that the only way she was going to be able to finish the conversation was if she followed him.

Knowing that a dive would definitely part her from the tiny bikini, she opted instead to use the ladder that hung from the back of the boat.

Sliding into the cooling water, she swam over to him.

Her confidence had increased a thousand times over the past few weeks, but was she really ready to go back to their old life?

She glanced up at the sky and, instead of being a perfect blue, it was grey and overcast.

And during the night the rain came.

Twenty-four hours later, Millie was back in London, reflecting on how much life could change in a few short weeks.

She looked in the mirror and for the first time ever she didn't wish that she could turn the lights down.

After two weeks alone with a flatteringly attentive Leandro, it was impossible not to feel beautiful.

Which was just as well because tonight they were going to be walking up the red carpet together. And there would be cameras.

To test her new confidence, Millie wore a dress of her own choosing, shoes that made her feel like a princess, and chose to leave her hair loose and curly.

Nestling against her throat was the heart-shaped diamond that Leandro had given her on their wedding day.

As she slipped her feet into her shoes, Leandro strolled into the dressing room.

He looked spectacular in a tailored dinner jacket and Millie felt a little pang as she realised that every woman in the room was going to be looking at him. For sheer visual impact there wasn't a man who came close to him, she thought weakly, and he caught her soft sigh and frowned.

'What are you thinking?'

'I'm wishing you weren't quite so attractive,' Millie said dryly. 'Then maybe women wouldn't all gape at you and I wouldn't feel so insecure.'

'After the past ten days I have no energy left,' he assured her in a silky tone, 'so you have no cause for concern.' He urged her out of the bedroom and down the stairs to the hallway. 'You look beautiful. You *know* you look beautiful.'

'I like hearing you say it.' Oblivious to the staff hovering, Millie wound her arms around his neck and he smiled and lowered his mouth to hers.

'Then I'll say it again,' Leandro murmured against her lips. 'You look beautiful.'

And she didn't argue because she saw it in his eyes when he looked at her.

'I didn't straighten my hair.'

'Good. I love your curls.'

'I've worn this dress before.'

'I know. I remember how good you looked in it the first time.'

'Do you think it makes my bottom look big?'

Leandro backed away from her, his hands spread in a defensive groan. '*Never* ask a man that question.' He laughed, but he turned her sideways and dutifully studied her rear view. 'It makes your bottom look like something out of a man's fantasy. And now I want to—'

'Don't you *dare* rumple me!' Wriggling away from the possessive slide of his hands, Millie couldn't help laughing. 'You're insatiable.'

'Yes. But unfortunately for me I am the guest of honour.' With a regretful sigh, he reached for his BlackBerry and made a quick call. 'Otherwise...' he returned the phone to his pocket '...I would feel the need to devote the rest of my evening examining the size of your bottom at close quarters. My driver is waiting outside for us.'

Millie walked towards the front door, but he stopped her.

'Wait—I have something for you.' His voice husky, Leandro reached into his pocket and retrieved a long black box. Opening it, he lifted out a slim, diamond bracelet.

Millie gasped and covered her mouth with her hands. 'Leandro, you can't—'

'I can.' He fastened it around her wrist and then stood back and narrowed his eyes. 'It suits you.'

'It matches my necklace.'

'Of course.' His hands firm on her shoulders, he turned her so that she could see her reflection in the hall mirror.

The diamonds sparkled against her creamy skin and she lifted a hand and touched them reverentially. 'I might get mugged.'

His jaw tightened and he drew her close. 'Never again,' he said gruffly. 'You're with me. And that's where you're staying. And I will protect you.'

As they stepped into the back of the luxurious car, Leandro spoke quietly to the driver and then turned to her. 'There will be media,' he warned her as they drew up outside the venue. 'Just smile.'

And she did.

Millie smiled her way up the red carpet, smiled at the cameras, smiled at the guests who gaped and jostled each other for an introduction, and she smiled at Leandro, who was as sexy as sin in his role of powerful tycoon. He slipped easily from one environment to another, she thought as she chatted casually to the man seated to her left.

She felt more confident, more at ease than she ever had before, and turned to Leandro with a grateful smile. 'I'm having a nice time.'

'Good.' His searing gaze rested on her cleavage. 'I'm not. All I want to do is take you home.'

Millie reached for her wineglass, enjoying the feeling of power that she had over him. The tension gradually mounted between them and by the time Leandro announced that they could leave, both of them were desperate.

They kissed in the car

As they approached the gates of his house, Millie noticed the hordes of press and her heart sank.

'What are they doing here? I thought they'd lost interest in us.'

'Ignore them.' A frown on his face, Leandro spoke to the driver in Greek and they were driven at speed through a network of roads which eventually brought them to the back of the house.

'I love this secret entrance.' Millie giggled, lifting the hem of her dress so that it didn't drag on the grass. 'It's so romantic. And I love the fact that the press haven't discovered it.'

'It's useful,' Leandro replied, but she sensed he was distracted by something. 'Come on. Let's go inside.'

They were greeted by the housekeeper, who was clearly agitated.

'I'm glad you're home—something terrible…' Nervously she rubbed her hands together and Millie felt her legs turn to jelly.

'Costas? Is he ill?' She stepped forward, panic making her legs shake. 'I shouldn't have gone out. Is something wrong with him?'

'The baby is fine, madam,' the housekeeper assured her, but the pity and embarrassment in her eyes made Millie drop back a few steps.

'Then what's wrong?'

'How anyone can write such stuff—do they have no shame?' Clearly distressed, the housekeeper blinked furiously. 'We've had all the papers put in the conservatory, Mr Demetrios, and I've instructed the staff that they're not to speak to anyone. The press have been knocking and calling, but we haven't answered. It's shameful, if you ask me, a man not being able to have peace in his own home.'

Without uttering a word, Leandro turned and strode towards the living room.

Feeling as though her shoes were lead weights, Millie followed him into the room and closed the door behind her. Even though she didn't know what was wrong, her heart was thudding and she felt sick with dread.

Even without looking, she knew that the newspapers would have done another hatchet job on her. But how? They'd only taken her photograph a few hours earlier.

Leandro picked up the first of the newspapers and scanned it briefly. The expression on his handsome face didn't alter as he threw it aside and picked up the next.

Almost afraid to look, Millie stooped and picked up one of the discarded copies. The Hollywood actress smiled seductively from the front page, and the caption read, 'Loving Leandro—my Unforgettable Night with my Greek Tycoon'.

Millie dropped the paper.

Her mouth was dry and her hands were shaking, but something made her pick up the next paper that he'd dropped. This time she read the copy.

'She's described your night together in minute detail.'

'She has a vivid imagination,' Leandro said flatly, picking up the last of the newspapers. 'They all say the same thing. Leave them. It's filth.' But as he scanned the final newspaper his expression did alter, as if something printed there was the final straw.

His mouth a flat, angry line, he quickly folded the paper but Millie reached forward and tugged it away from him, some masochistic part of her wanting to see what had upset him so much.

'Millie, no!' Leandro stepped forward to take it from her but not before she'd seen the pictures of herself in a bikini.

'Oh, my God.' Appalled and mortified, she felt like hiding under a rock. 'How did they—? We—'

'They must have had photographers near my island.' Leandro jabbed his fingers into his hair and cast her a shimmering glance of apology. 'This is *my* fault. I took you on that boat and I made you wear the bikini.'

'You didn't know there'd be a photographer nearby.' Millie gave a hysterical laugh. 'Where was he? On the back of a dolphin?'

Leandro undid his bow-tie and released his top button. 'I'm truly sorry.' He broke off and muttered something in Greek. 'I'll speak to my lawyers immediately. There may be something they can do.'

'It's already been done.' Her mouth dry, Millie stared at the photos and the close-up of her scars. Then she looked at the photographs of the actress taken from her latest film. The cruel positioning of the two photographs took her breath away. 'You can't undo this, Leandro. It's out there now. It will always be out there. And you can't blame them for making comparisons between me and the Hollywood actress—it's too good a story to miss, isn't it? The entire British public will now be asking themselves the same questions I asked myself—why would you choose me? And that's just going to keep on happening.' Her lips felt stiff and her brain numb as she stumbled towards the door. 'Excuse me. I need to check on Costas.'

'Millie—'

'I can't talk about this right now, I'm sorry. I need to be on my own. I need some time to get my head round it.' Without giving him time to intercept her, Millie shot from the room and took refuge in the nursery. She felt as though she'd been stripped naked and the sense of violation was worse than the vicious attack that had caused the scars in the first place.

Everyone across the country would be staring at those intimate photos and everyone would be making judgements.

As if in sympathy with her distress, Costas was screaming uncontrollably and Millie dismissed the nanny and lifted him out of his cot, holding him close, deriving comfort from his familiar warmth.

'There, angel. It's all right,' she whispered, 'I'm here now. It's all right. You're fine.'

'I'm so sorry,' the nanny apologised. 'I can't do anything with him. I think he's going down with something. He's been hot all evening and fretting.'

'It's OK, I'll sit with him,' Millie muttered, feeling the baby's forehead burning. 'You go to bed. There's no sense in everyone being awake.'

'Shall I stay while you get changed? I'd hate for him to ruin your dress.' The nanny looked at her pityingly and Millie realised that she knew about the papers.

Her face turned scarlet because she *hated* the thought of people pitying her. 'I don't care about the dress. You go to bed. Thanks.'

The girl hesitated and then quietly left the nursery.

Millie sat down in the chair, Costas in her lap, happy to hide away with the baby for a while. The alternative was facing Leandro, and she wasn't up to that at the moment.

She needed to get her thoughts straight.

'What a mess,' she murmured. 'You have no idea what a mess this is. Why can't people just mind their own business? Why do they love reading about trouble in other people's lives? I'm never buying a newspaper again on principle. I'm going to read gardening magazines. They don't hurt anyone.'

Exhausted by the demands of the conversation, Costas hiccoughed a few times and eventually drifted off to sleep on her shoulder.

As she laid him carefully in the cot, Millie stared down at him. She looked at the dark lashes and the dark hair and felt her stomach flip uncomfortably.

The gossip and speculation was endless.

It was always going to happen, wasn't it?

Maybe he wouldn't have affairs, but while she was with Leandro there was always going to be someone willing to sell him out for money, or point out her imperfections for an audience of millions to laugh at.

There would always be women willing to talk about their experiences in bed with him.

Millie dragged the chair next to the cot and flopped down into it, miserable, vulnerable and worried.

For half an hour she watched the baby sleep, checked his temperature and listened to his breathing.

* * *

Leandro stood in his study, his tension levels soaring into the stratosphere as he finished talking to his lawyers. The newspapers were strewn in front of him. Ordinarily he wouldn't have given any of them a first read, let alone a second, but this wasn't about him. It was about Millie. And he knew that today it was newspapers, but next week the celebrity magazines would pick up the story and it would run and run.

Thinking about Millie's fragile confidence, he wanted to punch something.

Being exposed to this wasn't fair on her, was it?

She was too sensitive.

He had no idea where she was now but, knowing Millie, he suspected she'd be curled up in an insecure heap somewhere, convinced that their relationship was never going to work.

His jaw tightened.

Perhaps she was right. Perhaps it never was going to work. Who on earth wanted to live with this?

Needing to do something to relieve his frustration, Leandro took the stairs to the top floor and pushed his way through the door that led to the secluded roof terrace.

Here, there were no cameras. No one watching.

Just the soothing rush of water from the fountain in the centre, the scent of plants, darkness and his thoughts.

He strolled to the balcony, from where he was able to see over the rooftops of London.

Up until this point in his life he'd been indifferent to the media intrusion. It hadn't bothered him. But now…

Millie was a living, breathing human being with feelings.

And those feelings had been badly hurt.

Leandro thought about those few seconds before they'd known what was wrong. Her thoughts had immediately been with the baby.

And when she'd seen those pictures of herself…

Guilt ripped through him, intense and unfamiliar as he dealt with the knowledge that he'd put her in a position that had allowed those pictures to be taken.

But the truth was that the media interest in his life was such that there would always be a photographer lurking, waiting to snap their picture. Even if he'd protected her from that one, he wouldn't necessarily have been able to protect her from the next.

And every time the press printed something nasty about her, another layer of her confidence would be shredded.

To be able to withstand the media you needed the hide of a rhinoceros, and Millie's flesh was as delicate as a rose petal.

She'd be torn, he thought grimly. *Ripped apart.*

And the decent thing would be to let her go—set her up somewhere new, where no one was interested in her.

From below in his courtyard he heard the roar of a car engine, but Leandro was too preoccupied to give it any thought.

Remembering that the last time he'd let Millie go had proved to be a mistake of gigantic proportions, Leandro strode back into the house and down the stairs, only to bump into the housekeeper, who was looking anxious and stressed.

'Don't tell me—more journalists?' Leandro spoke in a rough voice, a sinking feeling in the pit of his stomach. 'What's happened this time?'

'Millie has gone,' the woman told him. 'I heard her running through the house and then she said something like "No, don't do this to me" and then she took your car and drove like a maniac out of the drive. Gone. Just like that. She almost ran over the journalists waiting outside the gates.'

Gone. Crying.

Don't do this to me?

Remembering the roar of the car engine, Leandro's jaw tensed. 'Did any of the security staff follow her?' But he didn't need to see the appalled look on the housekeeper's face to know the answer to that one.

'It all happened so fast—'

Remembering what had happened the last time Millie had driven away from him upset, it took Leandro a moment to wrestle his emotions under control and think clearly.

He'd known she was upset but he'd given her the space she'd requested. And now he regretted it. He shouldn't have left her alone.

Leandro ran his fingers through his hair, his tension mounting as he thought of all the dangers she could now be facing. She was in London, alone and unprotected with a pack of press as hungry as hyenas. She was alone in his high-performance sports car in a cosmopolitan city where driving could be a life-threatening experience.

His expression grim, he strode into the house and walked straight to his study. Once there he contacted his head of security, gave him a brief and then proceeded to get slowly and methodically drunk.

After his third glass he discovered that there were some pains that alcohol couldn't numb, and he stopped drinking and closed his eyes.

How, he wondered, could he have made such a success of his life in every other area, and yet have made such a mess of his entire dealings with Millie?

Exhausted and anxious, Millie pushed the door open to Leandro's study.

Leandro lay sprawled in the chair, his dark hair rumpled, his shirt creased and his jaw shaded by stubble.

'Leandro?' Her voice was soft and tentative and he opened his eyes and looked at her.

Then he gave a hollow laugh. 'What did you forget?'

Thinking that it was a strange question, Millie gave him a rueful smile. 'Just about everything.' Not wanting to wake everyone else in the house, she closed the door quietly behind her. 'I was in such a state, I ran out of the house with nothing.'

'I know. The housekeeper heard you go.'

'You must have been a bit surprised.'

'Not really. Why would I be surprised? I know you were upset by everything. I understand that. What I don't understand is why you're back.'

Millie noticed the bottle and the empty glass by his hand. 'What are you talking about?' Confused, she took in his rumpled state and the lines of tiredness on his face. She'd never seen him anything other than immaculate before, neither had she seen him tired. He had endless energy and stamina. Only now he seemed spent. 'Why wouldn't I have come back?'

'I would have thought that was obvious.' Leandro growled. He lifted his glass to his lips and then realised that it was empty and put it down again.

Millie looked at him in exasperation. 'You're not making sense. And I don't know why you're getting drunk. I expect you're worried, but it's all going to be fine.'

'It is *not* going to be fine,' he said in a raw tone. 'This is going to keep happening.'

'No, they think it was just a one-off. It happens sometimes.'

'You're deluding yourself.'

Millie frowned, thinking that his comment was a little harsh. 'The doctor seemed to know what he was talking about.'

'Doctor?'

'That's where I took him. To the hospital.' She looked at

him defensively. 'Maybe I was overreacting, but I thought it might be life-threatening. I was so worried about him. What if I'd stayed here and he'd got worse? I looked for you and you'd disappeared. And after the stress and worry I've had this evening, I would have thought even you could be a little more sympathetic.' Hurt and not understanding his reaction, Millie turned away. 'I'm going to bed. I'm sleeping in Costas's nursery in case he needs me.'

'Wait a moment.' Leandro snapped out the words, his body still, his beautiful eyes narrowed to dark slits. 'What are you talking about? Why did you see a doctor? And why would Costas need you?'

'Because…' Millie was so tired that she couldn't even think straight and it took her a moment to absorb the implication of his question. 'Do you *honestly* not know what's been going on here? Where do you think I've been? Why do you think I dashed off?' She broke off and her breathing quickened as understanding dawned. 'Oh, my God, you thought I'd—'

'Yes,' he said softly. 'I did.'

Millie's heart started to pound. 'Why would you think that?'

'Do you really need to ask that question? The papers are full of my affair with that actress and extremely revealing pictures of you. Last time I saw you, you were upset.'

Millie walked across to him and stuck out her hand. 'Give me your phone.'

'I don't have it.' His voice was faintly mocking and a sardonic smile touched his mouth. 'Since you laid down your ground rules for our relationship I frequently lose track of where I've put it.'

'Well, isn't that typical of a man. The one time I need you to have your phone on you, you don't have it.' Bending over his desk, Millie shifted files and papers with scant regard for order and retrieved it from under a stack of papers. 'Here.' She thrust it towards him. 'I'm hopeless at technology. Switch it on.'

He switched it on.

Millie folded her arms. 'Now play back your messages. On speaker.'

Sending her a curious glance, Leandro played his messages.

Millie heard her own voice coming from the loudspeaker. *'Leandro, where are you? Costas is ill—I need to get him to a hospital. I'm taking your car. Call me when you get this message or meet me at the hospital.'*

Raising her eyebrows, Millie removed the phone from his hand. '*Now* I know why you didn't call. Really, you are going to have to be a bit more supportive when our own baby is born. If I'm going to have night-time panics, I want you with me. You're the one who is always calm in a crisis. I'm a mess. I'm never doing that again without you there to tell me that everything will be fine. What's the matter with you? I've never known you silent before. *Say* something.'

There was a long, tense silence during which Millie was sure she could hear her own heart beating.

When Leandro finally spoke, his voice was hoarse. '*Our* baby?'

'Yes. Our baby. I'm pregnant.' She gave a faint smile. 'Hardly surprising after all the sex we've had over the past few weeks.'

He inhaled sharply. 'Is that why you came back?'

'I never left,' Millie said softly, and Leandro held her gaze.

'Our baby.' He sounded stunned. 'All that stuff in the paper…'

Millie's heart missed a beat because everything she needed to know was in his voice and in his eyes. 'Well, I'm not pretending it wasn't upsetting. But I had plenty of time to think about it while I was watching over Costas in his cot. For a start, that actress is too thin for you. You hate women whose bones stick out. And you're forgetting, I was there that night. I could see that she was angry that you rejected her. The talk is that her latest film is rubbish. I expect she wanted to attract some different publicity—kick-start her career. And she wanted to hurt you.'

'It only hurts me if it hurts you,' Leandro said hoarsely, and then shook his head. 'I don't know why you're smiling. You like seeing me miserable?'

'No,' Millie said softly. 'I like seeing you in love.'

His eyes met hers. 'You're very confident all of a sudden.'

Millie shrugged and slid onto his lap. 'That happens when you're loved. And when you love back.' She leaned her head against his shoulder, feeling his strength. 'You should have known I wouldn't have left you.'

'Alexa said she saw you drive off, very upset.'

'I *was* very upset.' She sat up so that she could explain. 'I was sitting with Costas, just watching him, because I was worried about his temperature. And I was thinking about Becca—and us—and those awful pictures of me. Everything. And then Costas sort of went all floppy. I was terrified. I don't know. I'm not that experienced with children. He seemed so hot, and I was worried—'

'Why didn't you come and find me?'

'I did! You weren't here!' Millie was indignant. 'I ran around the house yelling your name but this house is so stupidly big and I couldn't find you. Neither could I find any of the staff.'

'I was up on the roof terrace. I needed fresh air.'

'Well, it's a shame you chose that particular moment because I was in desperate need of a serious dose of your

decisive-macho-Viking-invader approach to life. Leandro?'
She curled her hand into the front of his shirt. 'What is the
matter with you? I've never seen you like this before. You
look as though you have no idea what to do next, and you
always know what to do.'

Leandro slid his hand into her hair. 'Not always. Tonight I
thought I'd lost you forever and I had no idea what to do
about it. My first instinct was to find you and haul you back,
but I love you too much to involve you in the media circus that
is my life. It's always like this, Millie. There's always someone
wanting to sell me out to the media for money. And I blame
myself for those photos of you,' he confessed in a raw tone,
letting his hand drop so that she could see the look in his eyes.
'I should have known better than to expose you to that.'

'I don't care what they think,' Millie said softly. 'I only care
what *you* think.'

Leandro wrapped his arms around her. 'When you left the
first time, I was so angry. I'd thought you were the sort of
woman who would stay by my side no matter what. I didn't
understand how insecure you were and I didn't understand
how much my behaviour had dented your confidence. When
you were prepared to take on Costas, even though you still
thought he was my child—' He broke off, his eyes bright.
'That was when I realised that I didn't know you at all.'

'I found it impossible to believe that a man like you could
possibly want me.' Millie gave a wry smile. 'The media finds
it hard to believe, too, so you can't exactly blame me.'

'The media don't know you,' he said roughly. 'And I understand now why you felt that way. I understand why you would
have believed your sister.'

'I always just thought she was helping me.' Millie pulled
a face, unable to disguise the hurt. 'Stupid me.'

'Not stupid. Generous. You don't see bad in people. And why would you? She was your sister. I see how growing up with her must have made it hard for you to see your own qualities. But those qualities shine from you, *agape mou*. And those qualities are the reason I love you. I love your smile and your values, I love the way you were prepared to care for a child that might have been mine, and I love the way you still treasure the good memories of your sister, despite everything.' He inhaled deeply. 'And you're right when you say that I love you. I do. I loved you the first moment I saw your legs in that haystack.'

'That was lust, not love.'

A sexy smile tugged at his mouth. 'Perhaps, but it was love soon after. That's why I was so upset when you walked out. I thought I'd found a woman who would be by my side always.' His hand tightened on hers. 'I should have come after you.'

'If you'd known me better, maybe you would have done. And if I'd known you better, maybe I wouldn't have left.'

'I understand now why you did.' His hand slid into her hair in a possessive gesture. 'But at the time I thought you were like my mother.'

Millie stilled. 'You've never talked about your mother. You've never talked about your family at all.'

'Because I try to keep that part of my life in the past, where it belongs. I built myself a new life.' His voice was husky. 'She left me. When I was six years old—old enough to understand rejection—she went out one day and left me with a friend of hers. And she never came back.'

'Leandro—'

'She was a single mother and life was tough.' He gave a weary shrug. 'I think she just woke up one day and thought life might be easier without the burden of a young child.'

Millie didn't know what to say so she just leaned forward and hugged him. 'Where did you go?'

'I was taken back to Greece and put into care. But I found it hard to attach myself to anyone after that. If your own mother can leave you, why wouldn't a stranger?'

'Why didn't you tell me this before?'

'I thought I'd put it all behind me, but scars don't always heal, do they?'

'But you can learn to live with scars,' Millie said softly, tasting her own salty tears as she pressed her mouth to his. 'If you can live with mine, I'll teach you to live with yours.'

His hand slid into her hair and tightened, as if he were holding on. 'You're sure you want this life?'

'I want to spend my life with you. You've given me so many things, Leandro. Diamonds, houses, cars, a lifestyle beyond my wildest dreams, but the most important thing you've given me is self-esteem. You make me feel special.'

'You *are* special.' He cupped her face in his hands. 'You took on your sister's child, despite everything.'

'So did you.' Millie's eyes filled. 'You took him on knowing that he wasn't yours. Knowing that everyone would make assumptions.'

'I didn't want Costas to go through what I went through.' He gave a twisted smile. 'The situation was different, I know, but for me it felt like a healing process. I was able to give this baby a home, a name—an identity. Everything I never had. Millie…' He was hesitant. 'This lifestyle isn't going to change. If you stay with me, there are always going to be people hunting you down, wanting to make you believe bad things about me.'

Millie leaned forward and kissed him. 'Is this a good moment to confess that I might need the services of your lawyer after all?'

'Why?'

She shrank slightly. 'I was in a panic when I put Costas in your car…'

'And…?'

'I think I might have accidentally damaged one of the motorcycles that the journalists had propped against your gate. It was in the way. I was also responsible for the fact that one of the journalists dropped his camera.'

'Sounds like you need driving lessons.' Laughter in his eyes, Leandro raised an eyebrow in mocking contemplation. 'Dare I enquire after the health of my Ferrari?'

Millie squirmed. 'It's nice to know where your priorities lie. It might need a teeny-weeny touch of paint.'

Leandro closed his eyes. 'I don't love you any more.'

Millie giggled and wound her arms round his neck. 'Yes, you do.'

'You're right, I do.' Leandro took her face in his hands and kissed her. 'I love you, *agape mou*. I will always love you, no matter how many Ferraris you get through or how many journalists sue me. You say that you're different to every other woman I've ever been with and that's true—you are. That's why I fell in love with you. I saw instantly that you were different. You weren't interested in my money and you had values that I admired and respected.'

'I can see why you were disappointed when you thought I'd turned into a shopaholic.'

'I didn't look for a reason for the change in your behaviour. I accused you of not trusting me, but I was guilty of that charge, not you. I assumed you'd suddenly discovered how much you enjoyed having the money.'

'Leandro, I *do* like the money,' Millie muttered. 'Anyone would be mad not to, wouldn't they? I love the fact that I don't have to queue for a bus in the rain. I'll never stop being thrilled when the lights turn on by themselves, but most of all I love the fact I'm going to be able to stay at home with Costas and our baby and not work.'

'Bab*ies,*' Leandro purred, his characteristic arrogance once more in evidence. 'I intend to keep you very busy in that department. I'd hate Costas to be lonely.'

Millie grinned. 'This one isn't cooked yet.'

He slid his hand over her flat stomach in a gesture that was both intimate and protective. 'You will be a fantastic mother.'

Millie kissed him, feeling the roughness of his jaw against her sensitive skin. 'What are we going to do about Costas? I can't bear to think of him growing up with this question of his parentage hanging over him.'

'My lawyers have started adoption proceedings,' Leandro told her. 'I can't pretend it's going to be a quick and simple process, but we'll get there, I promise you that. We're his parents.'

'And I think we should have a couple of dogs. Big dogs. Trained to bite journalists.'

Leandro laughed. 'I was so wrong about you. I used to think you were gentle and kind.'

'I am, most of the time. As long as no one upsets me.' Millie grinned. 'It's no good frowning. You don't scare me any more.'

'I'd noticed. In fact, I'm not sure I like the new, confident you,' he drawled. 'I'm not sure you know your place.'

Millie wound her arms round his neck. 'I know my place, Leandro Demetrios,' she said softly, and he lifted an eyebrow in question.

'So where is your place, *agape mou?*'

'By your side, bearing your children, loving you for the rest of my life. That's my place.'

And Leandro smiled his approval just moments before he kissed her.

HARLEQUIN *Presents*

EXTRA

Presents Extra brings you
two new exciting collections!

MISTRESS BRIDES

*When temporary arrangements
become permanent!*

The Millionaire's Rebellious Mistress #85
by CATHERINE GEORGE

Da Silva's Mistress #86
by TINA DUNCAN

MEDITERRANEAN TYCOONS

At the ruthless tycoon's mercy

Kyriakis's Innocent Mistress #87
by DIANA HAMILTON

The Mediterranean's Wife by Contract #88
by KATHRYN ROSS

Available January 2010

www.eHarlequin.com

HPE0110R

HARLEQUIN *Presents*

TWO CROWNS, TWO ISLANDS, ONE LEGACY

A royal family torn apart by pride and its lust for power, reunited by purity and passion

THE ROYAL HOUSE *of* KAREDES

Harlequin Presents is proud to bring you the final two installments from The Royal House of Karedes. As the stories unfold, secrets and sins from the past are revealed and desire, love and passion war with royal duty!

Look for:

RUTHLESS BOSS, ROYAL MISTRESS
by Natalie Anderson
January 2010

THE DESERT KING'S HOUSEKEEPER BRIDE
by Carol Marinelli
February 2010

www.eHarlequin.com

HP12883

HARLEQUIN *Presents*

AT HIS *Service*

From glass slippers to silk sheets

Once upon a time there was a humble housekeeper.
Proud but poor, she went to work for a charming and
ruthless rich man!

She thought her place was below stairs—
but her gorgeous boss had other ideas.

Her place was in the bedroom, between his
luxurious silk sheets.

Stripped of her threadbare uniform, buxom and blushing
in his bed, she'll discover that a woman's work has never
been so much fun!

Look out for:

POWERFUL ITALIAN,
PENNILESS HOUSEKEEPER
by India Grey
#2886
Available January 2010

www.eHarlequin.com

HP12886

REQUEST YOUR FREE BOOKS!

2 FREE NOVELS
PLUS 2
FREE GIFTS!

YES! Please send me 2 FREE Harlequin Presents® novels and my 2 FREE gifts (gifts are worth about $10). After receiving them, if I don't wish to receive any more books, I can return the shipping statement marked "cancel". If I don't cancel, I will receive 6 brand-new novels every month and be billed just $4.05 per book in the U.S. or $4.74 per book in Canada. That's a savings of close to 15% off the cover price! It's quite a bargain! Shipping and handling is just 50¢ per book*. I understand that accepting the 2 free books and gifts places me under no obligation to buy anything. I can always return a shipment and cancel at any time. Even if I never buy another book, the two free books and gifts are mine to keep forever.

106 HDN EYRQ   306 HDN EYR2

Name _____ (PLEASE PRINT) _____

Address _____ Apt. # _____

City _____ State/Prov. _____ Zip/Postal Code _____

Signature (if under 18, a parent or guardian must sign) _____

Mail to the **Harlequin Reader Service:**
IN U.S.A.: P.O. Box 1867, Buffalo, NY 14240-1867
IN CANADA: P.O. Box 609, Fort Erie, Ontario L2A 5X3

Not valid to current subscribers of Harlequin Presents books.

Are you a current subscriber of Harlequin Presents books and want to receive the larger-print edition? Call 1-800-873-8635 today!

* Terms and prices subject to change without notice. Prices do not include applicable taxes. Sales tax applicable in N.Y. Canadian residents will be charged applicable provincial taxes and GST. Offer not valid in Quebec. This offer is limited to one order per household. All orders subject to approval. Credit or debit balances in a customer's account(s) may be offset by any other outstanding balance owed by or to the customer. Please allow 4 to 6 weeks for delivery. Offer available while quantities last.

Your Privacy: Harlequin Books is committed to protecting your privacy. Our Privacy Policy is available online at www.eHarlequin.com or upon request from the Reader Service. From time to time we make our lists of customers available to reputable third parties who may have a product or service of interest to you. If you would prefer we not share your name and address, please check here. ☐

HARLEQUIN
Ambassadors

Want to share your passion for reading Harlequin® Books?

Become a Harlequin Ambassador!

Harlequin Ambassadors are a group of passionate and well-connected readers who are willing to share their joy of reading Harlequin® books with family and friends.

You'll be sent all the tools you need to spark great conversation, including free books!

All we ask is that you share the romance with your friends and family!

You'll also be invited to have a say in new book ideas and exchange opinions with women just like you!

To see if you qualify* to be a Harlequin Ambassador, please visit www.HarlequinAmbassadors.com.

*Please note that not everyone who applies to be a Harlequin Ambassador will qualify. For more information please visit www.HarlequinAmbassadors.com.

Thank you for your participation.

I ♥ HARLEQUIN Presents